D0309296

LIBRARIES NI
WITHDRAWN FROM STOCK
LIBRARIES NI
WITHDRAWN FROM STOCK

GRAPHICS

EGMONT

We bring stories to life

First published in Great Britain 2016
by Egmont UK Limited, The Yellow Building,
1 Nicholas Road, London W11 4AN.

Direction: Catherine Saunier-Talec
Editorial and artistic director: Antoine Béon
Project Manager: Anne Vallet
Illustrations: Bunka
Production: The business office graphics
Monitoring: Nicolas Beaujouan
Manufacturing: Amélie Latsch

© & TM 2016 Lucasfilm Ltd.

ISBN 978 1 4052 7636 8
59021/1
Printed in Spain by Graficas Estella

All rights reserved. No part of this publication may be reproduced, stored in a retrieval system, or transmitted in any form or by any means, electronic, mechanical, photocopying or otherwise, without the prior consent of the copyright owner.

Stay safe online. Egmont is not responsible for content hosted by third parties.

To find more great *Star Wars* books, visit www.egmont.co.uk/starwars

STAR WARS™

GRAPHICS

A LONG TIME AGO IN A GALAXY
FAR, FAR AWAY....

TABLE OF CONTENTS

GENERAL INFORMATION

FIRST TRILOGY

SECOND TRILOGY

GENERAL INFORMATION

[1977-2005]

BESPIN

Biosphere :
gas, clouds
Diameter :
118,000 km
Natives :
Neo-Bespinians
Population :
6 million
Films :
Episodes V & VI

KAMINO

Biosphere :
oceans
Diameter :
19,270 km
Natives :
Kaminoans
Population :
1 million
Film :
Episode II

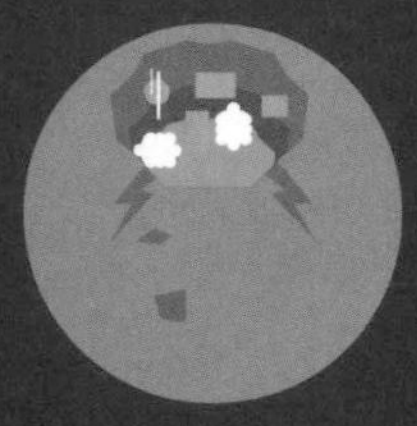

UTAPAU

Biosphere :
desert
Diameter :
12,900 km
Natives :
Utapauns
Population :
95 million
Film :
Episode III

KASHYYYK

Biosphere :
forests, plains
Diameter :
12,765 km
Natives :
Wookiees
Population :
45 million
Film :
Episode III

ALDERAAN

Biosphere :
forests, lakes, mountains
Diameter :
12,500 km
Natives :
Killiks
Population :
2 billion
Films :
Episodes III & IV

CORUSCANT

Biosphere :
urban
Diameter :
12,240 km
Natives :
humans
Population :
1 trillion
Films :
Episodes I, II, III & VI

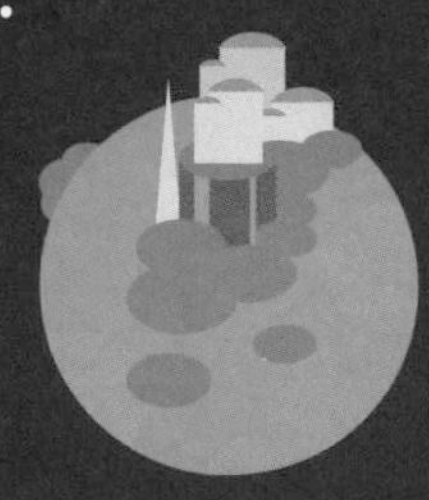

NABOO

Biosphere :
plains, lakes
Diameter :
12,120 km
Natives :
Gungans
Population :
4.5 billion
Films :
Episodes I, II, III & VI

GEONOSIS

Biosphere :
rock, deserts, mountains
Diameter :
11,370 km
Natives :
Geonosians
Population :
100 billion
Film :
Episode II

TATOOINE

Biosphere:
deserts
Diameter:
10,465 km
Natives:
Tuskens
Population:
80,000
Films:
Episodes I, II, III, IV & VI

YAVIN 4

Biosphere:
forests
Diameter:
10,200 km
Natives:
Colonised
Population:
0–1000
Film:
Episode IV

MYGEETO

Biosphere:
ice
Diameter:
10,088 km
Natives:
Lurmens
Population:
19 million
Film:
Episode III

FELUCIA

Biosphere:
mushroom forests
Diameter:
9,100 km
Natives:
Felucians
Population:
8.5 million
Film:
Episode III

DAGOBAH

Biosphere:
swamps
Diameter:
8,900 km
Natives:
Hepsalum Tash
Population:
1
Films:
Episodes V & VI

HOTH

Biosphere:
ice
Diameter:
7,200 km
Natives:
Skels
Population:
unknown
Film:
Episode V

ENDOR

Biosphere:
forests
Diameter:
4,900 km
Natives:
Ewoks
Population:
30 million
Film:
Episode VI

MUSTAFAR

Biosphere:
lava, volcanoes
Diameter:
4,200 km
Natives:
Mustafarians
Population:
20,000
Film:
Episode III

"BUT WHICH WAS DESTROYED, THE MASTER OR THE APPRENTICE?" MACE WINDU ASKED YODA AT THE END OF *THE PHANTOM MENACE*. HERE IS A DIAGRAM WHICH WILL HELP YOU UNDERSTAND WHO TAUGHT WHAT TO WHOM.

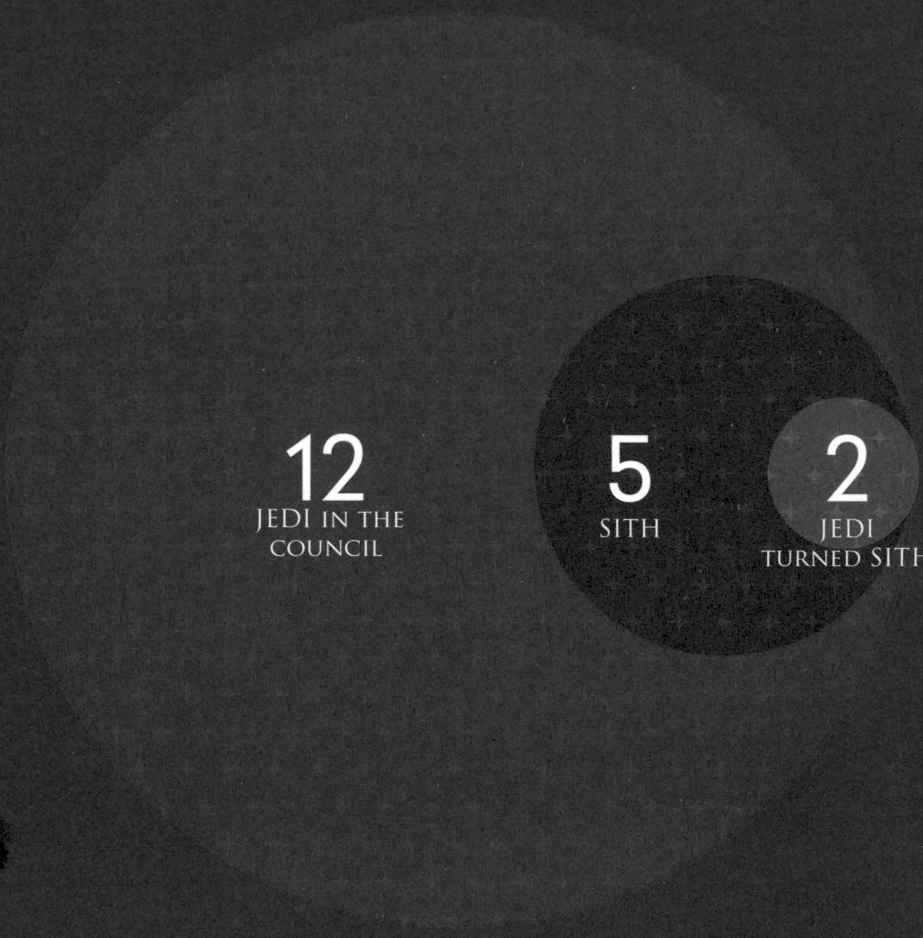

12
JEDI IN THE COUNCIL

5
SITH

2
JEDI TURNED SITH

BBY - Before the Battle of Yavin

ABY - After the Battle of Yavin

Birth: 147–120 BBY
Death: 32 BBY
Species: Muun
Planet: Mygeeto

DARTH PLAGUEIS

MASTER: Darth Tenebrous
APPRENTICE: Darth Sidious

FILM(S)

I II III IV V VI

Birth: 82 BBY
Death: 4 ABY
Species: human
Planet: Naboo

1.78 m
75 kg

DARTH SIDIOUS

MASTER: Darth Plagueis
APPRENTICES: Darth Maul, Darth Tyranus, Darth Vader

FILM(S)

I II III IV V VI

Birth: 54 BBY
Death: 32 BBY
Species: Dathomirian
Planet: Dathomir

1.75 m
80 kg

DARTH MAUL

MASTER: Darth Sidious
APPRENTICE: Savage Opress

FILM(S)

I II III IV V VI

Birth: 102 BBY
Death: 19 BBY
Species: human
Planet: Serenno

1.93 m
80 kg

DARTH TYRANUS

MASTERS: Yoda, Darth Sidious
APPRENTICES: Qui-Gon Jinn, Asajj Ventress (dark Jedi), Savage Opress (dark Jedi)

FILM(S)

I II III IV V VI

Birth: 41 BBY
Death: 4 ABY
Species: human
Planet: Tatooine

2.02 m
136 kg

DARTH VADER

MASTER: Darth Sidious
APPRENTICE: ?

FILM(S)

I II III IV V VI

Birth: 41 BBY
Death: 4 ABY
Species: human
Planet: Tatooine

♂
1.88 m
84 kg

ANAKIN SKYWALKER

MASTERS: Obi-Wan Kenobi, Ki-Adi-Mundi
APPRENTICE: Ahsoka Tano

FILM(S)

I II III IV V VI

Birth: Unknown
Death: 19 BBY
Species: Dathomirian / Zabrak Iridonian
Planet: Nar Shaddaa
1.71 m

EETH KOTH

MASTER: Kosul Ayada
APPRENTICE: Sharad Hett

FILM(S): I, II

Birth: 72 BBY
Death: 19 BBY
Species: human
Planet: Haruun Kal
1.88 m
84 kg

MACE WINDU

MASTERS: Yoda, T'ra Saa
APPRENTICES: Depa Billaba, Devan For'deschel, Echu Shen-Jon, Darrus Jeht

FILM(S): I, II, III

Birth: Unknown
Death: 19 BBY
Species: human
Planet: Chalacta
♀
1.68 m

DEPA BILLABA

MASTER: Mace Windu

FILM(S): I, II

Birth: 92 BBY
Death: 19 BBY
Species: Cerean
Planet: Cerea
1.98 m
82 kg

KI-ADI-MUNDI

MASTERS: An'ya Kuro, Yoda
APPRENTICES: A'Sharad Hett, Anakin Skywalker, Dama Montalvo, Tarr Seirr

FILM(S): I, II, III

Birth: 896 BBY
Death: 4 ABY
Species: Unknown
Planet: Unknown
66 cm
17 kg

YODA

MASTER: N'Kata Del Gormo
APPRENTICES: Count Dooku, Mace Windu, Cin Drallig, Ikrit, Qu Rahn, Rahm Kota, Obi-Wan Kenobi, Kit Fisto, Ki-Adi-Mundi, Oppo Rancisis, Luke Skywalker

FILM(S): I, II, III, V, VI

Birth: Unknown
Death: 19 BBY
Species: Iktotchi
Planet: Iktotch
1.88 m

SAESEE TIIN

MASTER: Omo Bouri

FILM(S): I, II, III

PLO KOON

Birth: 392 BBY
Death: 19 BBY
Species: Kel Dor
Planet: Kel Dor

♂ 1.88 m 80 kg

MASTER: Tyvokka
APPRENTICES: Bultar Swan, Lissarkh

FILM(S)

I | II | III

YARAEL POOF

Birth: Unknown
Death: 27 BBY
Species: Quermian
Planet: Quermia

♂ 2.64 m

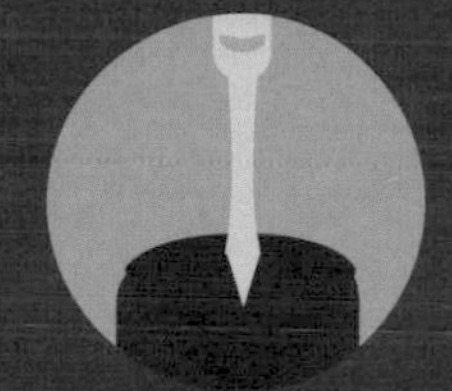

APPRENTICE: Roron Corobb

FILM(S)

I

OPPO RANCISIS

Birth: 206 BBY
Death: 19 BBY
Species: Thisspiasian
Planet: Thisspias

♂ 1.38 m

MASTERS: Yaddle, Yoda

FILM(S)

I | II

ADI GALLIA

Birth: Unknown
Death: 20 BBY
Species: Tholothian
Planet: Coruscant

♀ 1.84 m 50 kg

APPRENTICE: Siri Tachi

FILM(S)

I | II

YADDLE

Birth: 509 BBY
Death: 26 BBY
Species: Unknown
Planet: Unknown

♀ 61 cm

MASTER: Polvin Kut
APPRENTICES: Oppo Rancisis, Empatojayos Brand

FILM(S)

I

EVEN PIELL

Birth: Unknown
Death: 21 BBY
Species: Lannik
Planet: Lannik

♂ 1.22 m

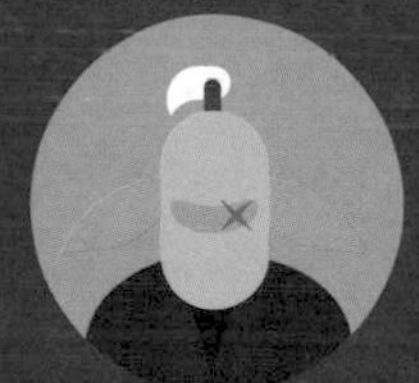

APPRENTICE: Jax Pavan

FILM(S)

I | II

JEDI VS SITH

THE DEADLY STRUGGLE BETWEEN THE SITH AND THE JEDI IS THE FOUNDATION ON WHICH THE *STAR WARS* UNIVERSE IS BUILT. HERE ARE THE MOMENTS WHERE YOU CAN SEE IT HAPPEN BEFORE YOUR VERY EYES.

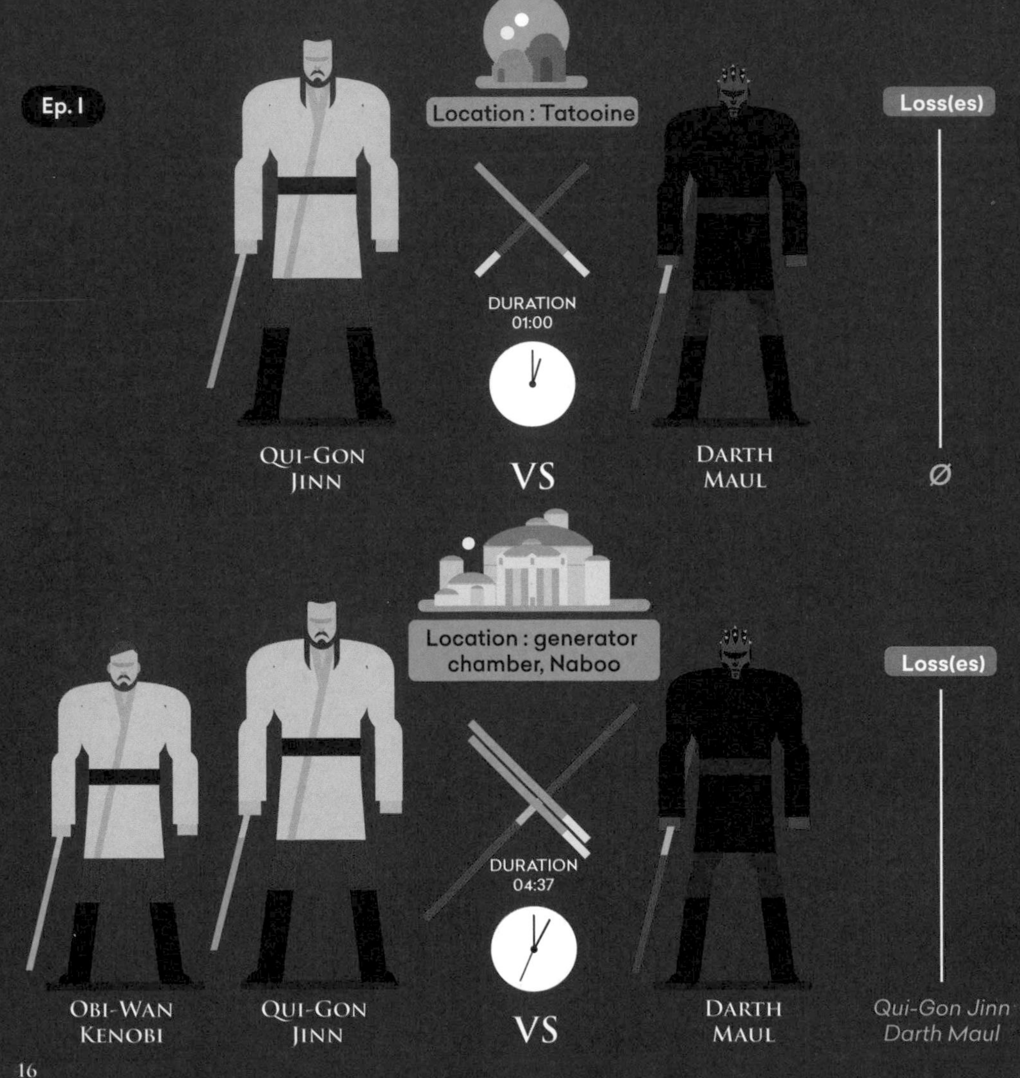

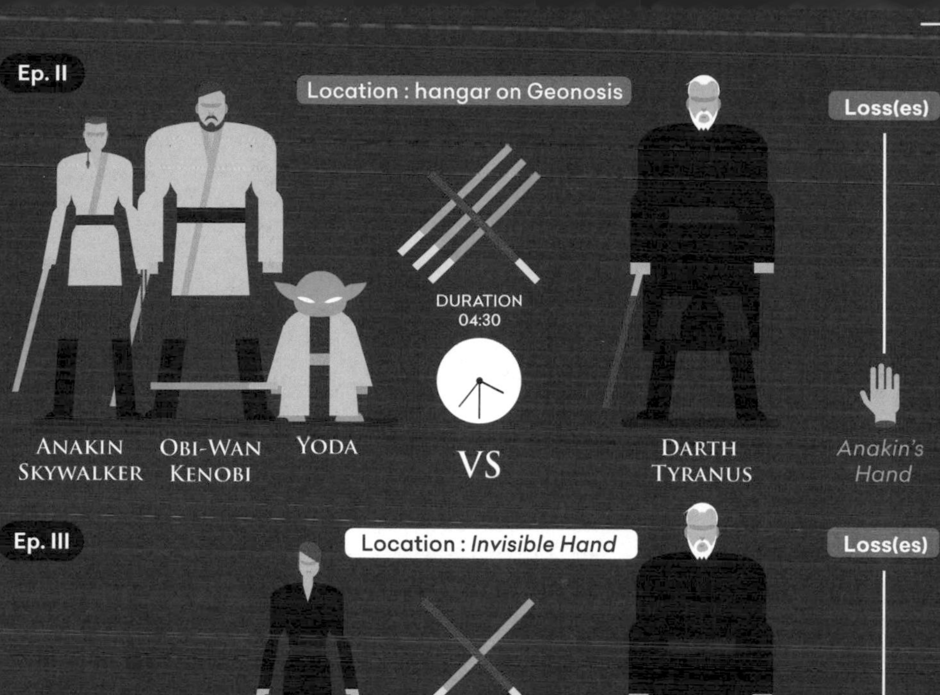
Ep. II
Location : hangar on Geonosis
Loss(es)
DURATION
04:30
ANAKIN SKYWALKER
OBI-WAN KENOBI
YODA
VS
DARTH TYRANUS
Anakin's Hand

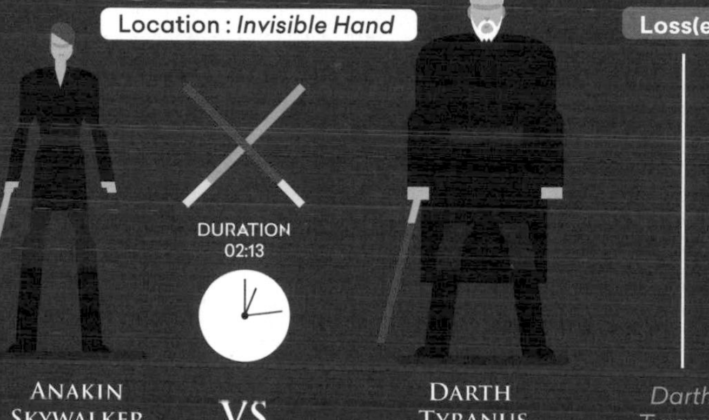
Ep. III
Location : Invisible Hand
Loss(es)
DURATION
02:13
ANAKIN SKYWALKER
VS
DARTH TYRANUS
Darth Tyranus

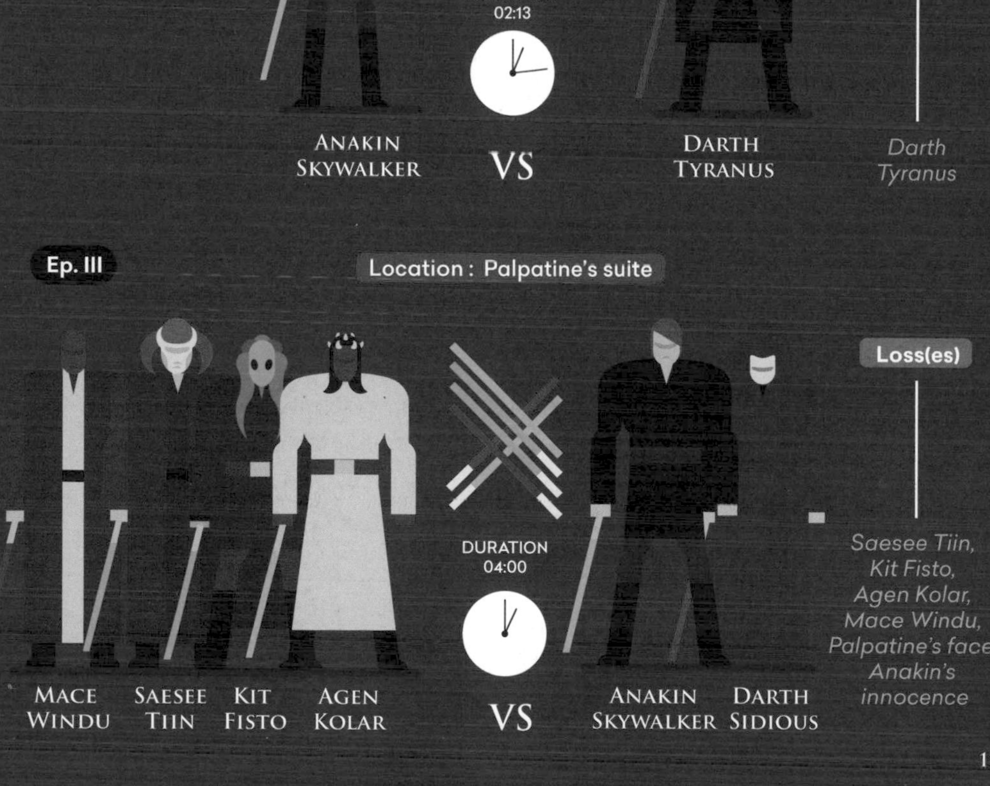
Ep. III
Location : Palpatine's suite
Loss(es)
DURATION
04:00
MACE WINDU
SAESEE TIIN
KIT FISTO
AGEN KOLAR
VS
ANAKIN SKYWALKER
DARTH SIDIOUS
Saesee Tiin, Kit Fisto, Agen Kolar, Mace Windu, Palpatine's face, Anakin's innocence

Ep. III

Loss(es)

∅

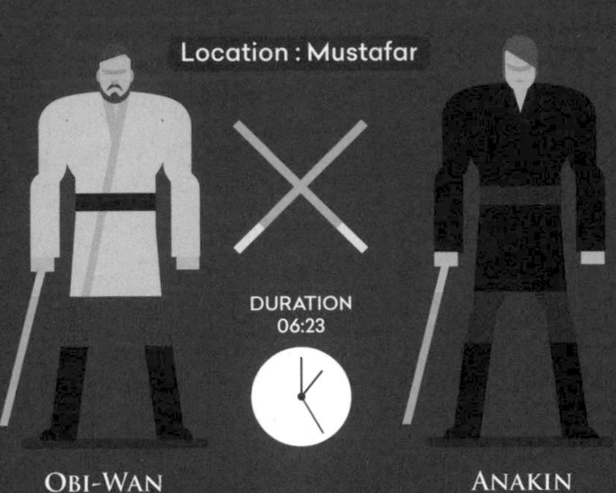

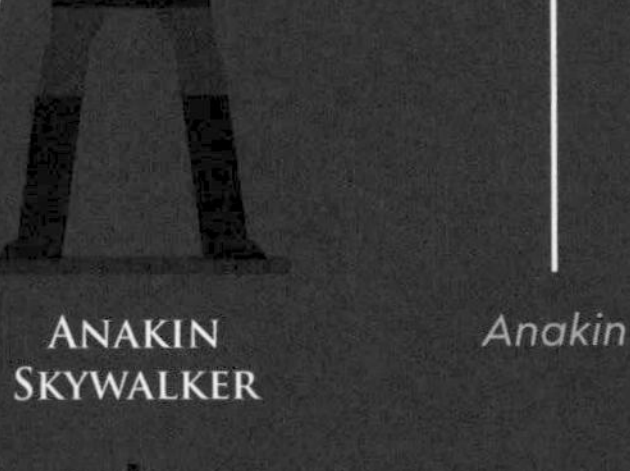

Loss(es)

Anakin

Ep. IV

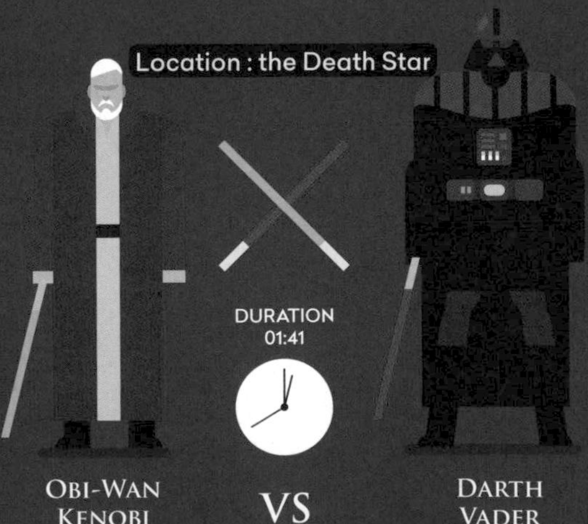

Loss(es)

Obi-Wan

Ep. V

Location : Dagobah

DURATION
00:20

LUKE SKYWALKER VS LUKE SKYWALKER

Loss(es)

Luke's innocence

Location : Cloud City

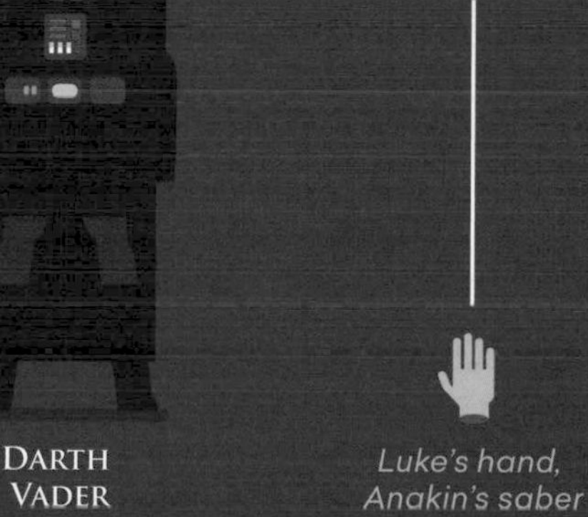

DURATION
06:40

LUKE SKYWALKER VS DARTH VADER

Loss(es)

Luke's hand,
Anakin's saber

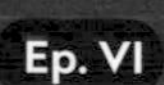

Location : Death Star II

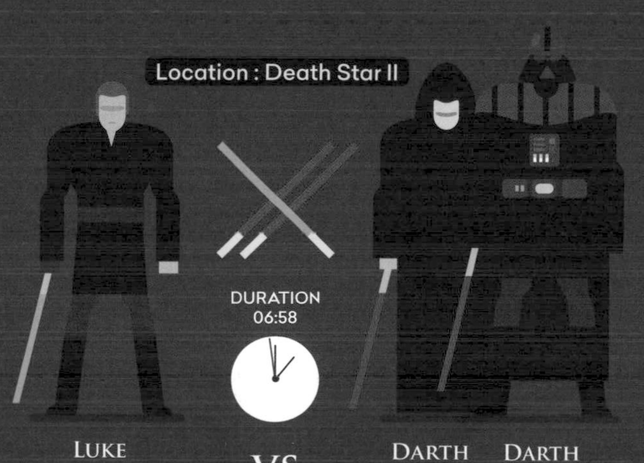

DURATION
06:58

LUKE SKYWALKER VS DARTH SIDIOUS DARTH VADER

Loss(es)

Darth Sidious,
Darth Vader's hand,
Darth Vader

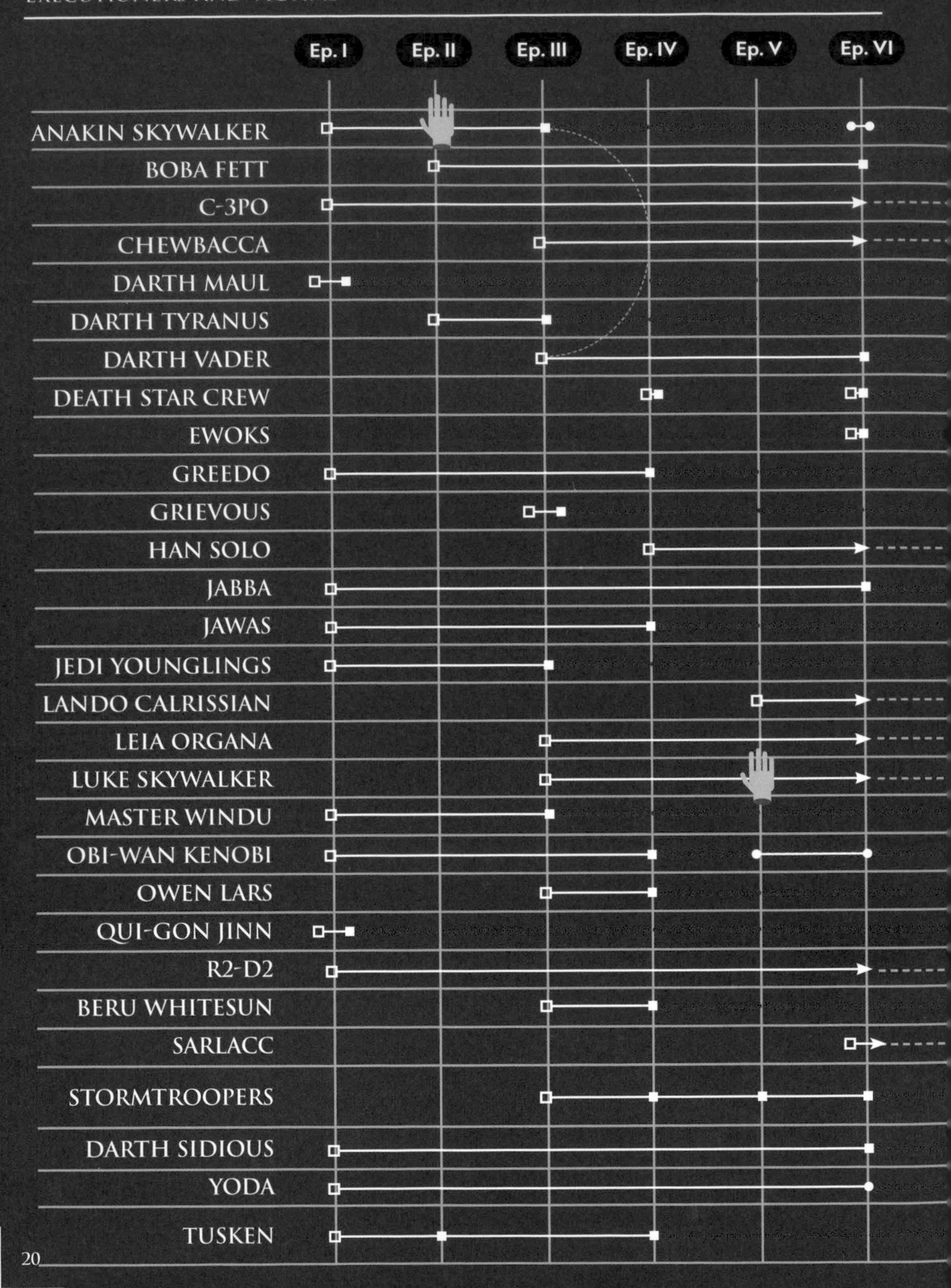
Ep. I
Ep. II
Ep. III
Ep. IV
Ep. V
Ep. VI
ANAKIN SKYWALKER
BOBA FETT
C-3PO
CHEWBACCA
DARTH MAUL
DARTH TYRANUS
DARTH VADER
DEATH STAR CREW
EWOKS
GREEDO
GRIEVOUS
HAN SOLO
JABBA
JAWAS
JEDI YOUNGLINGS
LANDO CALRISSIAN
LEIA ORGANA
LUKE SKYWALKER
MASTER WINDU
OBI-WAN KENOBI
OWEN LARS
QUI-GON JINN
R2-D2
BERU WHITESUN
SARLACC
STORMTROOPERS
DARTH SIDIOUS
YODA
TUSKEN

EXECUTIONERS AND VICTIMS

Appearance
Death
Reappearance
Life

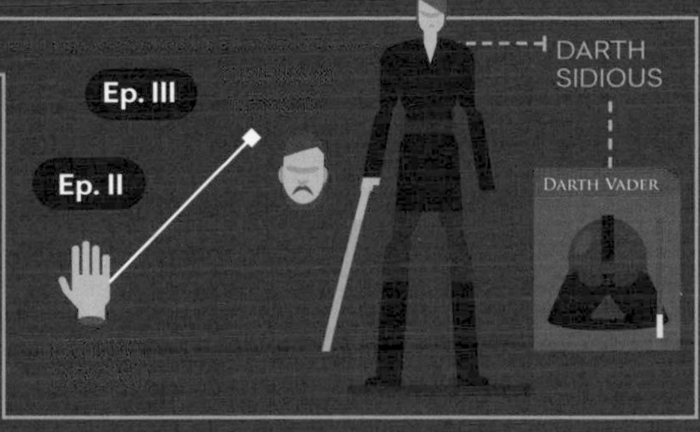

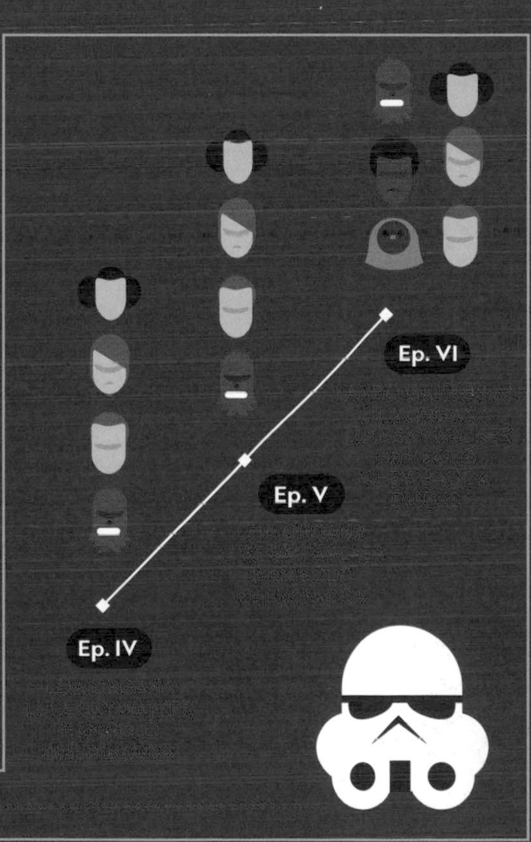

Ep. II
Ep. VI

LIGHTSABERS

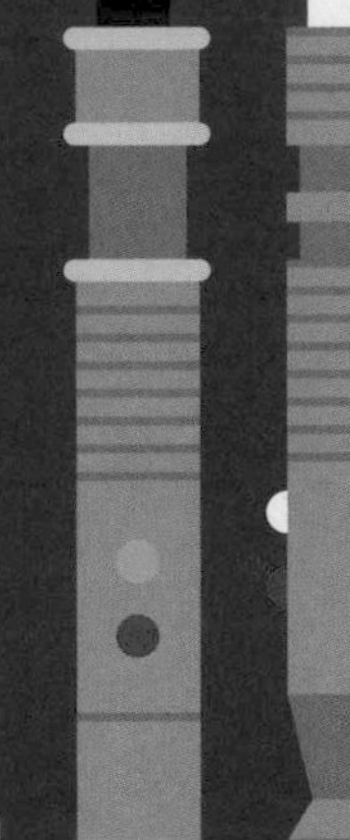
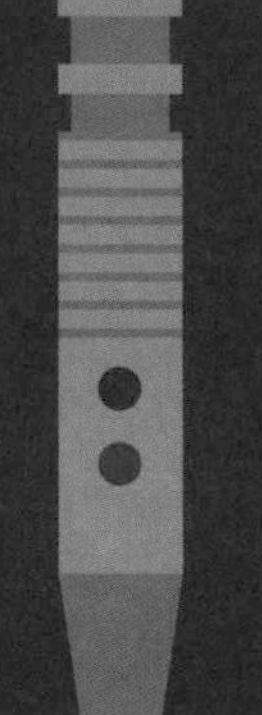

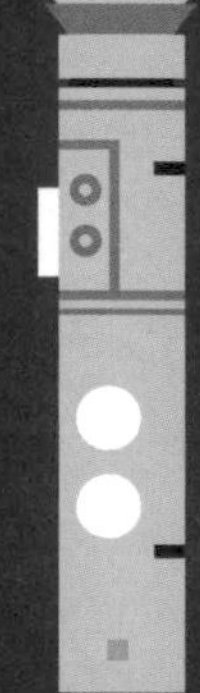

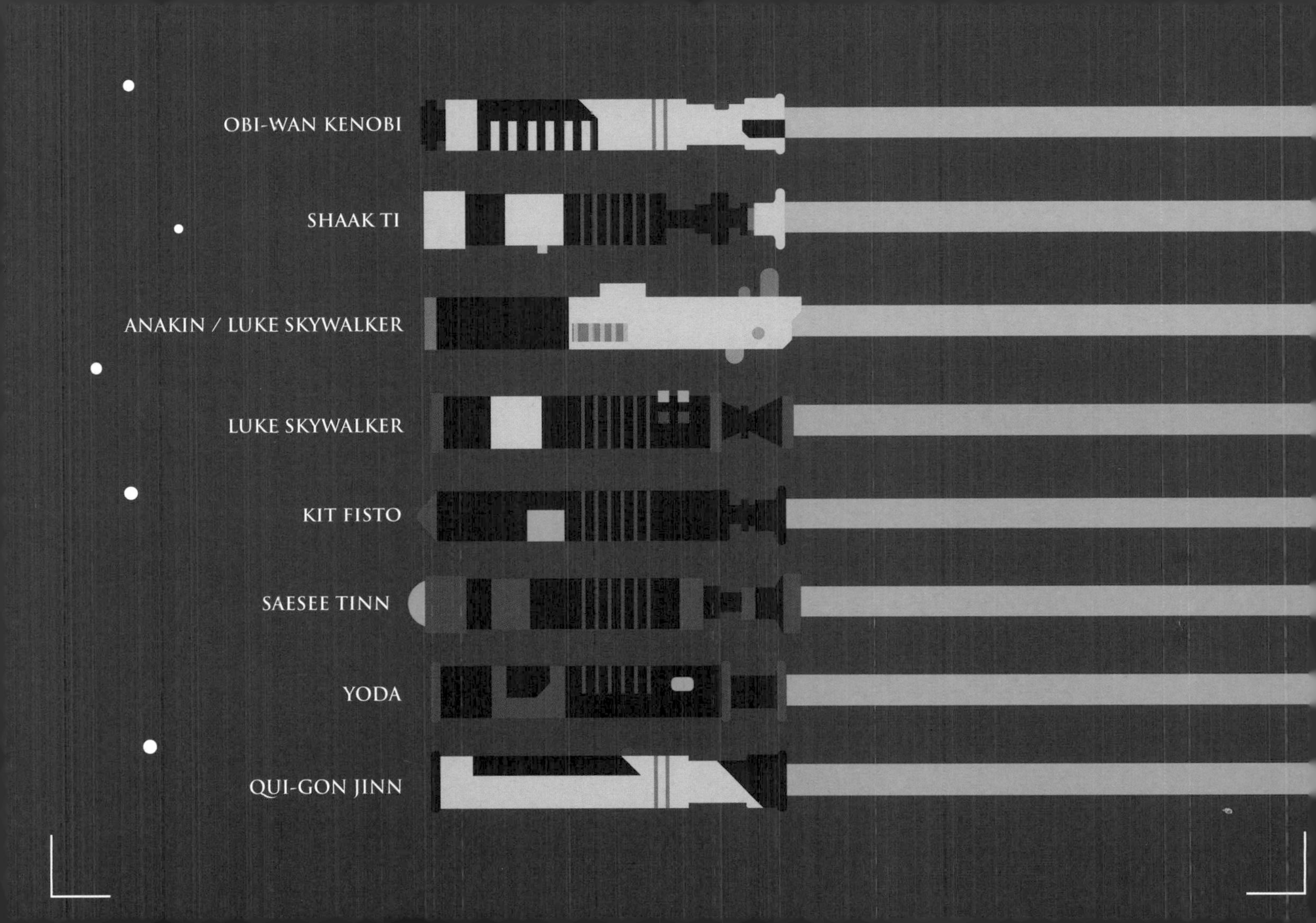

OBI-WAN KENOBI

SHAAK TI

ANAKIN / LUKE SKYWALKER

LUKE SKYWALKER

KIT FISTO

SAESEE TINN

YODA

QUI-GON JINN

Classification of Vessels According to Their Speed

PLATOON ATTACK CRAFT
FEDERATION — I

- 112 B1 droids, or 20 droidekas

50 Km/h

74-A SPEEDER BIKE
EMPIRE — VI

- AX-20m blaster cannon

500 Km/h

LANDSPEEDER
NEUTRAL — IV

250 Km/h

50 100 150 200 250 300 350 400 450 500

OG-9 HOMING SPIDER DROID
FEDERATION — II

- Mounted laser rifle
- Antipersonnel laser cannon
- Retractable ion cannon

80 Km/h

AT-AT
EMPIRE — V / VI

- 2 Taim & Bak MS-1 laser cannons
- 2 FF-4 repeating blasters
- Durasteel/Transport footpads
- 5 speeder bikes, 2 AT-ST/40 troopers

60 Km/h

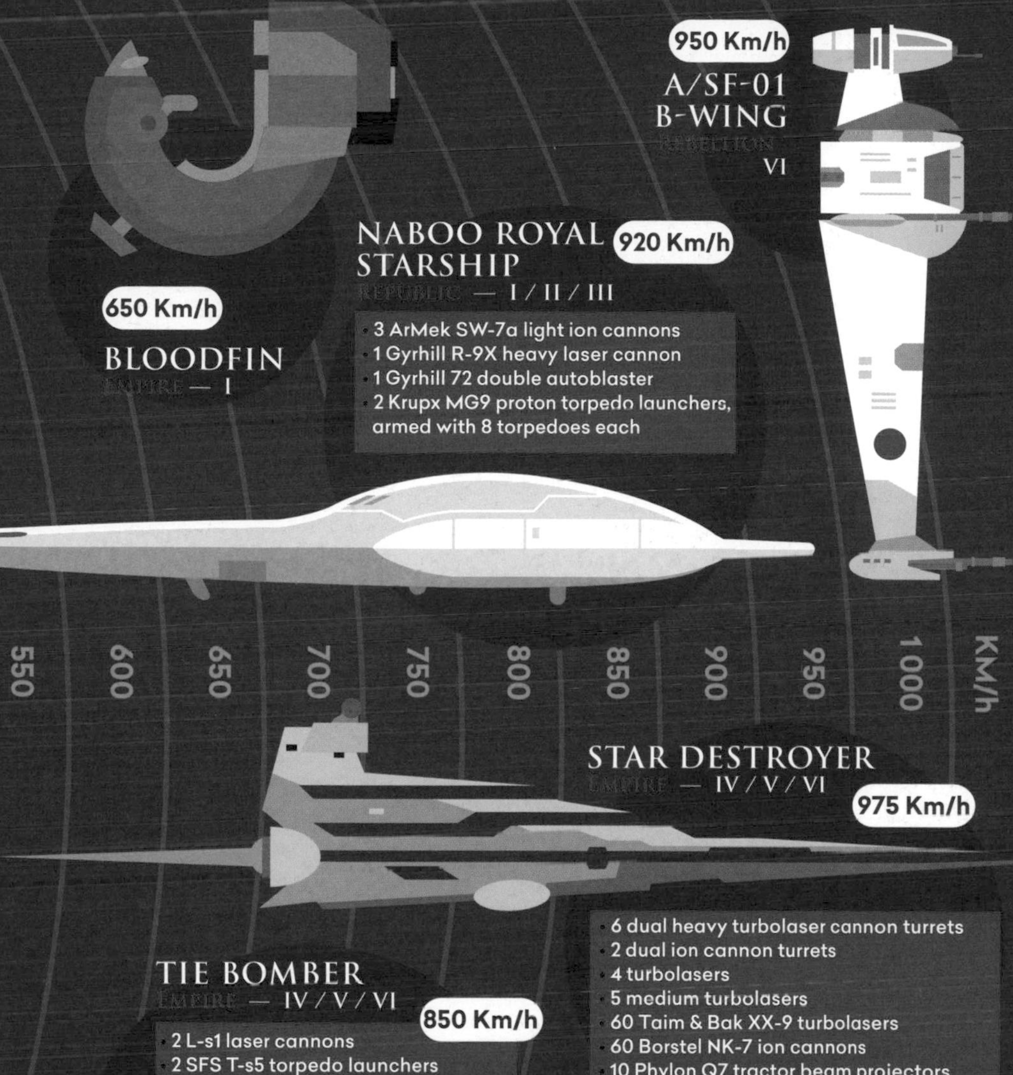

- 3 ArMek SW-7a light ion cannons
- 1 Gyrhill R-9X heavy laser cannon
- 1 Gyrhill 72 double autoblaster
- 2 Krupx MG9 proton torpedo launchers, armed with 8 torpedoes each

- 6 dual heavy turbolaser cannon turrets
- 2 dual ion cannon turrets
- 4 turbolasers
- 5 medium turbolasers
- 60 Taim & Bak XX-9 turbolasers
- 60 Borstel NK-7 ion cannons
- 10 Phylon Q7 tractor beam projectors
- 48 TIE fighters
- 12 TIE bombers
- 12 TIE transports
- 8 Lambda transport shuttles
- 15 Delta transports
- 5 assault ships
- 1 Gamma assault shuttle
- Maintenance vehicles
- AT-AT Theta barges
- 12 Sentinel transports
- 20 AT-AT, 30 AT-ST/9,235 officers
- 9700 troopers
- 27,850 reserves
- 275 gunners

TIE BOMBER

EMPIRE — IV / V / VI

850 Km/h

- 2 L-s1 laser cannons
- 2 SFS T-s5 torpedo launchers (4 torpedoes)
- 2 SFS M-s3 concussion missile launchers (8 missiles)
- 1 hold containing ArmaTek SJ-62/68 orbital mines
- ArmaTek VL-61/79 proton bombs
- Thermal detonators

Classification of vessels according to their speed

1000 Km/h

SLAVE I

NEUTRAL — II / V / VI

(Boba Fett version)

- 2 GN-40 twin rotating blasters
- 2 HM-8 concussion mortars
- 1 C/In ion cannon
- 2 AA/SL torpedo launchers armed with 3 torpedoes each
- 1 F1 tractor beam
- 1 scrambler launcher
- 9 Void-7 seismic mines

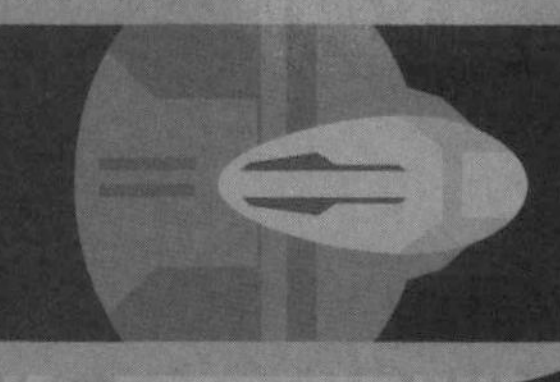

1200 Km/h

VULTURE DROID STARFIGHTER

FEDERATION — I / II

- 6 blaster cannons
- 2 energy torpedo launchers

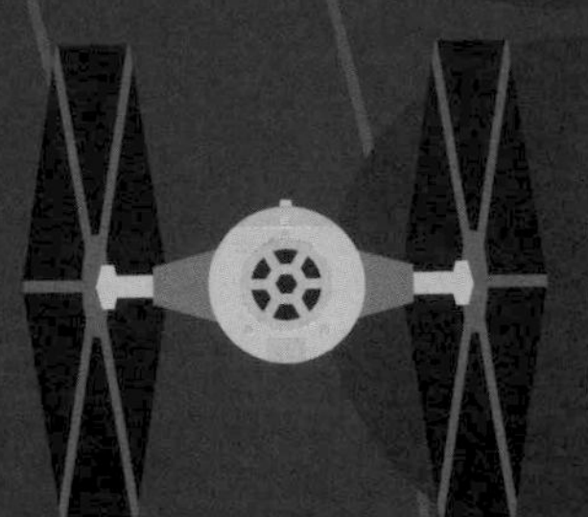

1200 Km/h

TIE FIGHTER

EMPIRE — IV / V / VI

- 2 laser cannons

1000 1050 1100 1150 1200 1250

1050 Km/h

X-WING

REBELLION — IV / V / VI

- 4 laser cannons
- 1 proton torpedo launcher

1050 Km/h

MILLENNIUM FALCON

REBELLION — IV / V / VI

1000 Km/h

BTL Y-WING

REBELLION — VI

- 2 KX5 or Taim & Bak IX4 laser cannons
- 2 turret-mounted SW-4 ArMek ion cannons
- 2 Arakyd FlexTube proton torpedo launchers armed with 4 torpedoes each
- Proton bombs

1200 Km/h

ACCLAMATOR-CLA TRANSGALACTIC

REPUBLIC — II

- 12 quadruple turbolaser cannons
- 24 laser cannons
- 4 proton mortars
- 16,000 clone troopers + crew

RZ1 A-WING

1 300 Km/h

REBELLION — IV / V / VI

- 2 Borstel RG-9 laser cannons
- 2 Dymek HM-6 concussion missile launchers armed with 6 missiles each

COUNT DOOKU'S SOLAR SAILER

1 600 Km/h

FEDERATION — II

- 84 tractor/repulsor beams

1350 1400 1450 1500 1550 1600 KM/h

ANSPORT

300 Km/h

-WING

EPUBLIC — I / II / III

- 3 laser cannons
- 1 proton torpedo launcher
- 16 torpedoes

DELTA-7 AETHERSPRITE LIGHT INTERCEPTOR

1 500 Km/h

REPUBLIC — III

- 2 laser cannons
- 2 ion cannons

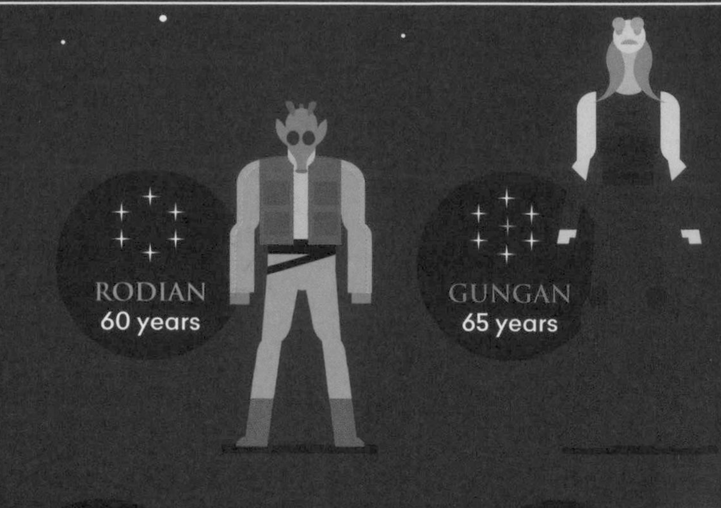
RODIAN
60 years
GUNGAN
65 years

EWOK
Up to 70 years

TAUNTAUN
90 years

WOOKIEE
More than 400 years

YODA
SPECIES UNKNOWN!
Up to 900 years

HUTT
More than 1,000 years

Life Expectancy in the Galaxy Far, Far Away

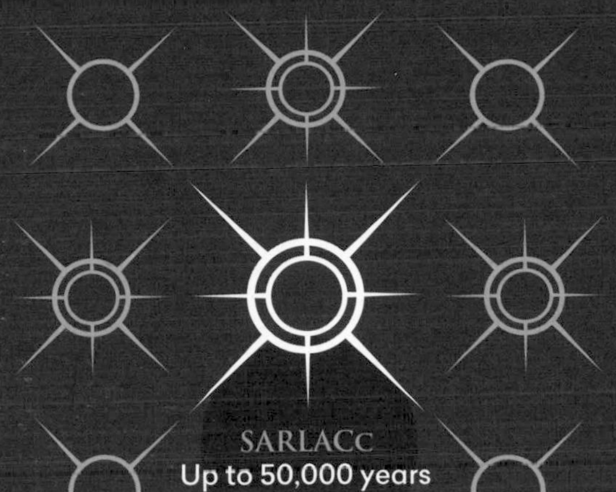

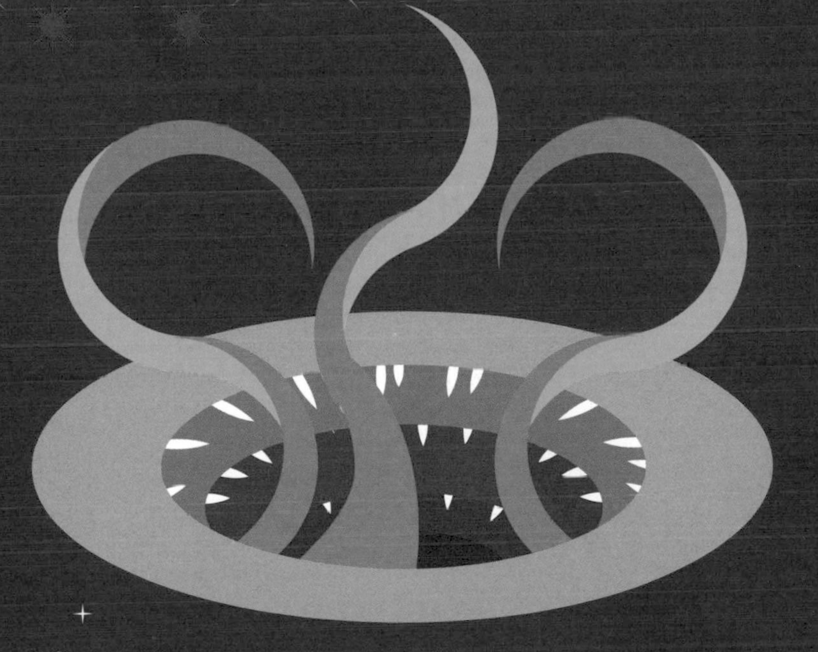

5 years

10 years

50 years

100 years

1,000 years

10,000 years

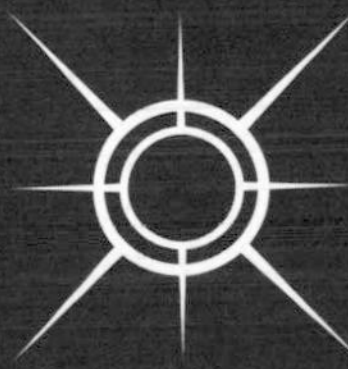

15,000 years

LOVE IN THE STARS

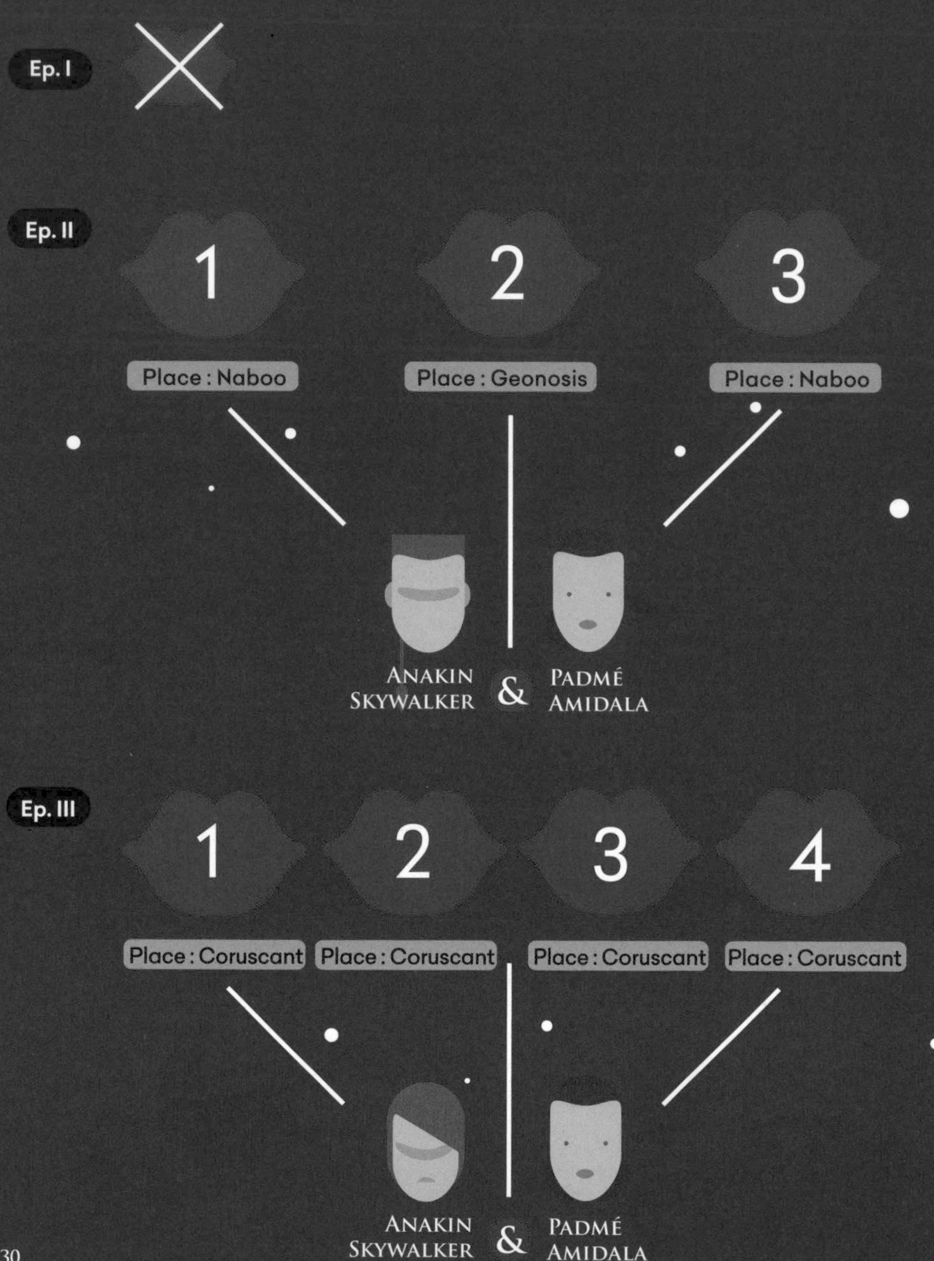

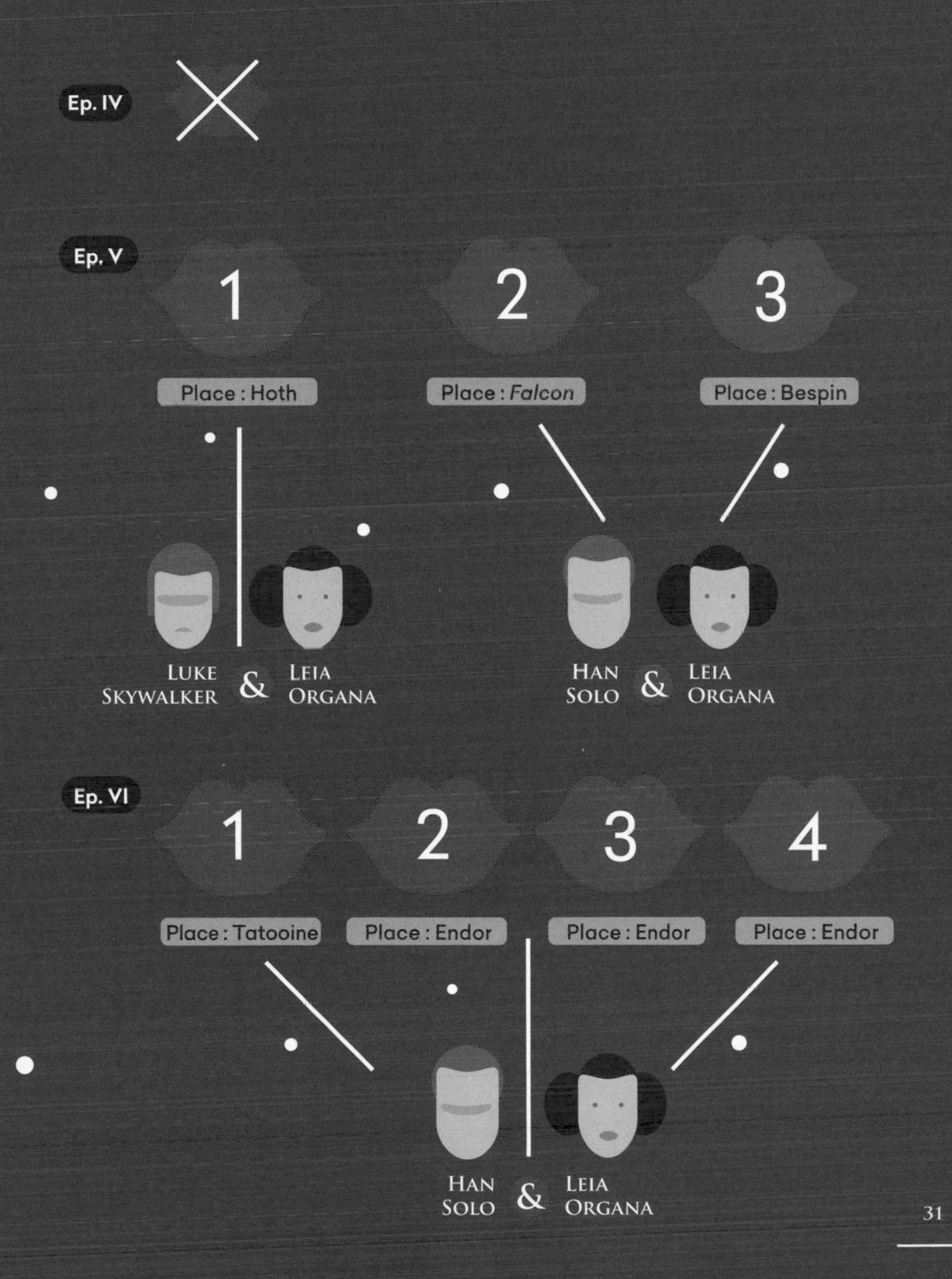
Ep. IV
Ep. V
1
2
3
Place : Hoth
Place : Falcon
Place : Bespin
Luke Skywalker & Leia Organa
Han Solo & Leia Organa
Ep. VI
1
2
3
4
Place : Tatooine
Place : Endor
Place : Endor
Place : Endor
Han Solo & Leia Organa

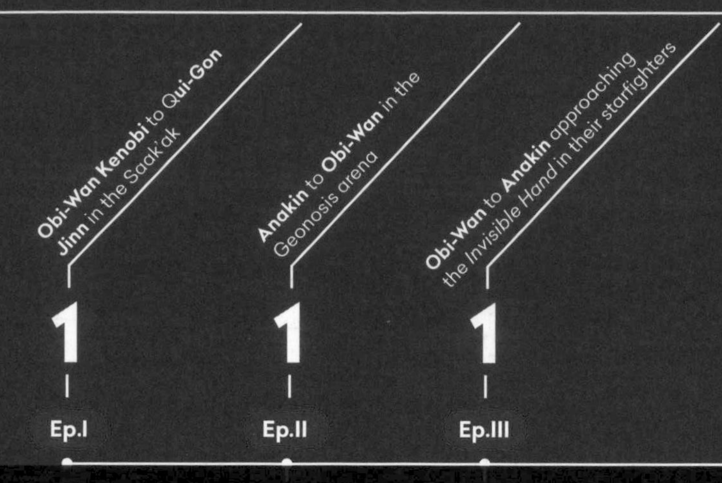

'I HAVE A BAD FEELING ABOUT THIS' 8 V

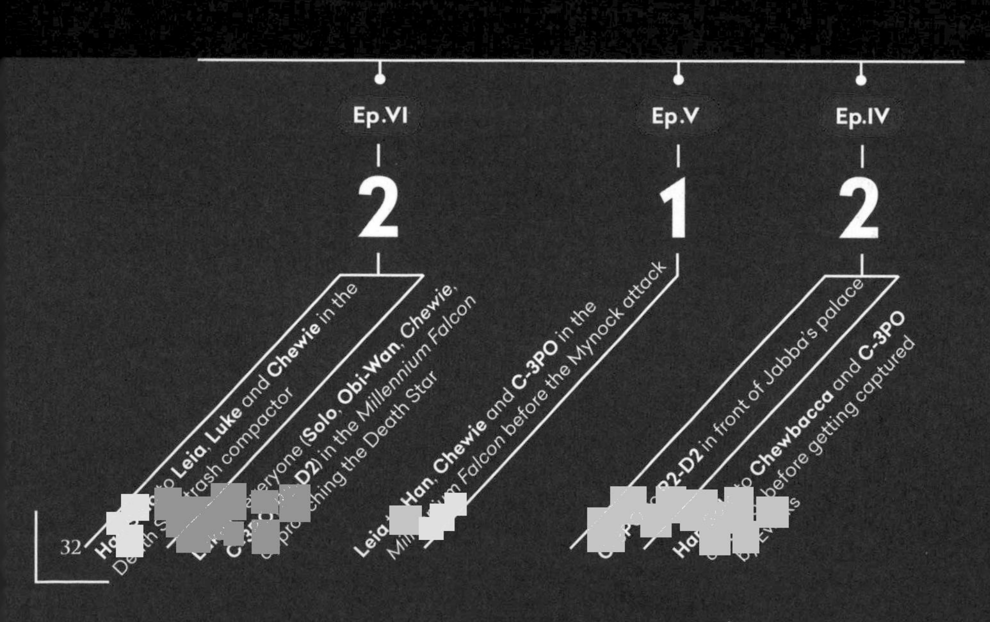

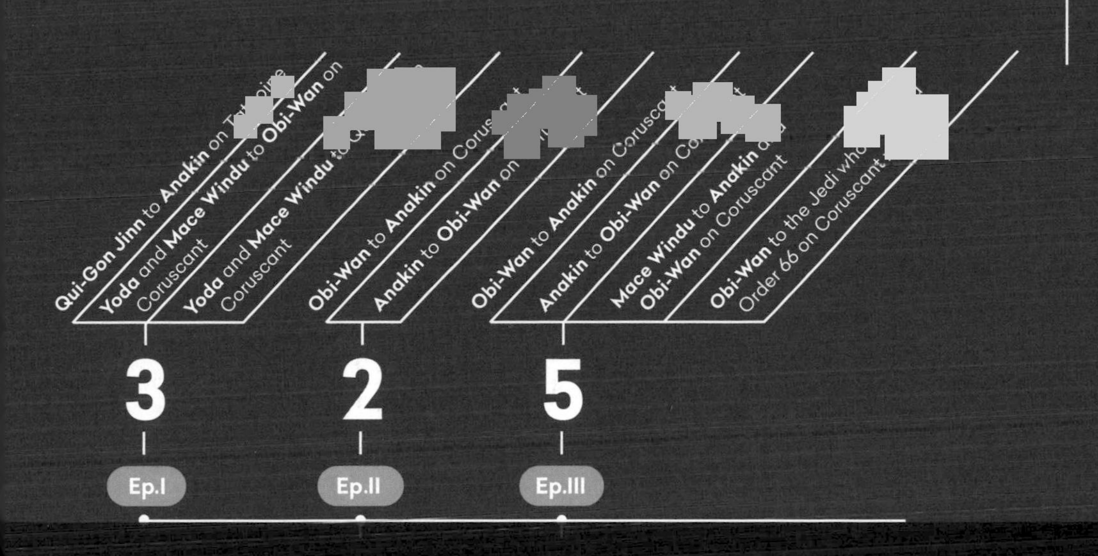

14 'MAY THE FORCE BE WITH YOU'

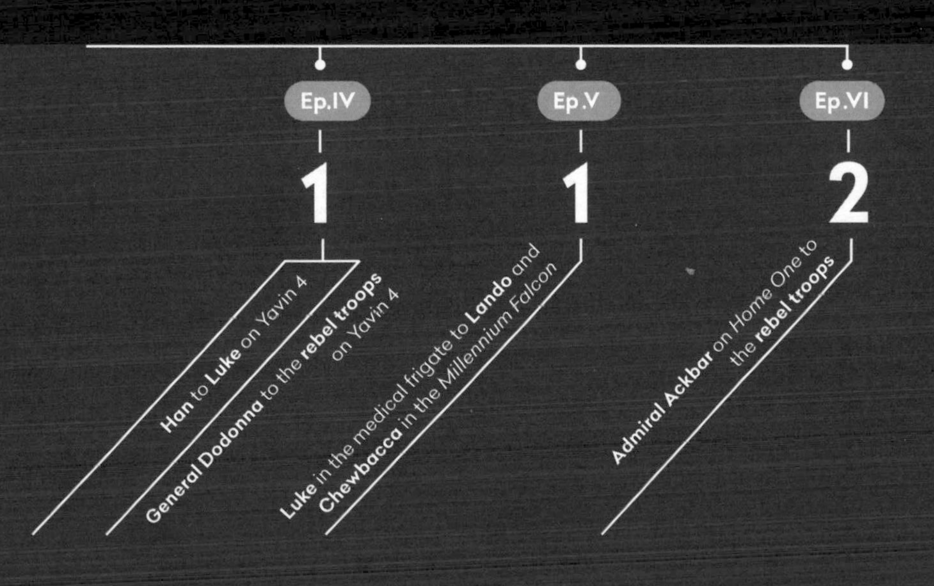

A LOT OF CHARACTERS LOSE BODY PARTS IN THE STAR WARS STORY. HUMANS, ALIENS, DROIDS, JEDI, SITHS – BE IT INTENDED OR UNINTENDED – ALL ARE AT RISK.

Ep. I DARTH MAUL

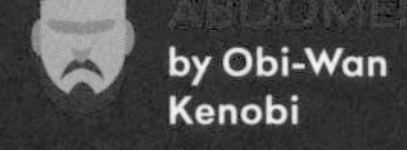

ABDOMEN
by Obi-Wan Kenobi

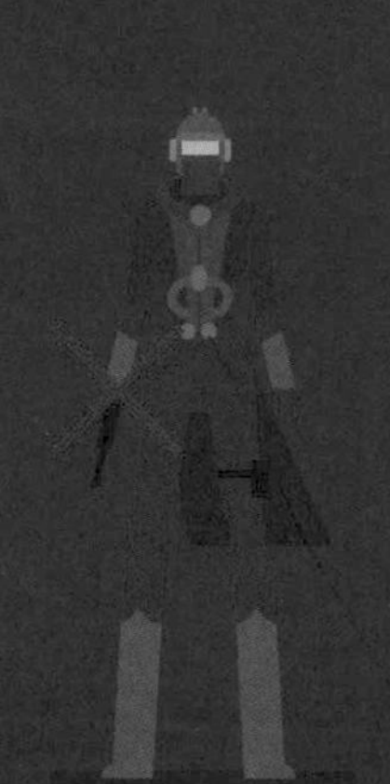

Ep. II ZAM WESELL

RIGHT HAND
by Obi-Wan Kenobi

Ep. II JANGO FETT

HEAD
by Mace Windu

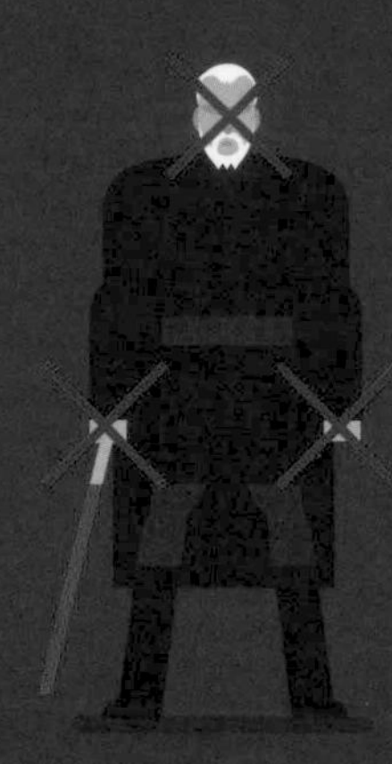

Ep. III COUNT DOOKU

HANDS AND HEAD
by Anakin Skywalker

C-3PO

Ep. II HEAD
by a factory robot

Ep. IV RIGHT ARM
by a Tusken Raider

Ep. V ALL HIS LIMBS

Ep. VI AN EYE
by Salacious Crumb

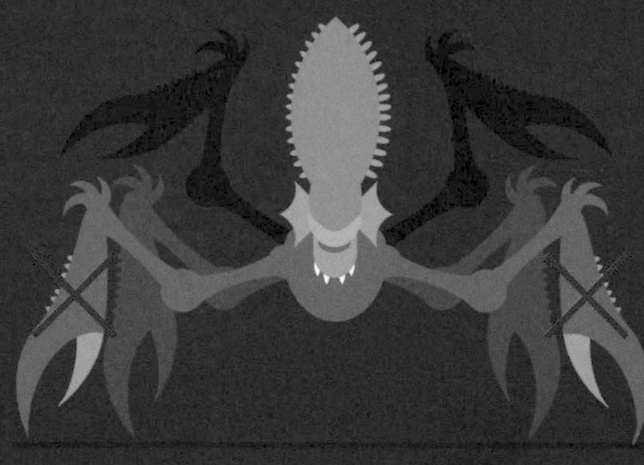

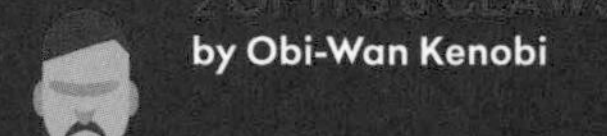

Ep. II ACKLAY

2 OF ITS 6 CLAWS
by Obi-Wan Kenobi

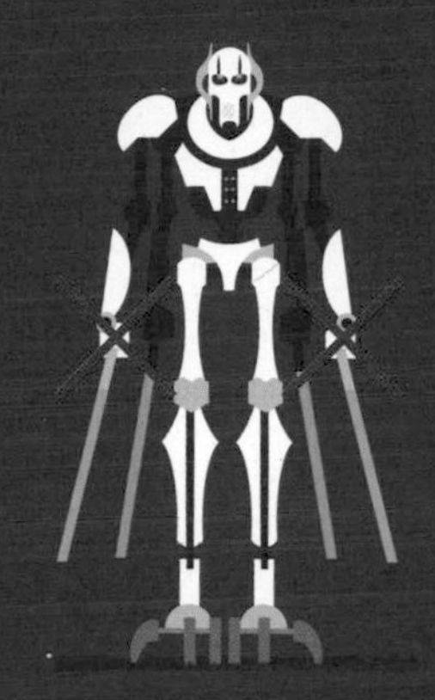

Ep. III **GENERAL GRIEVOUS**

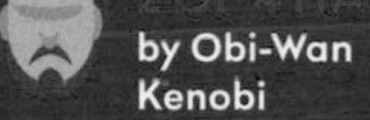

2 OF 4 HANDS

by Obi-Wan Kenobi

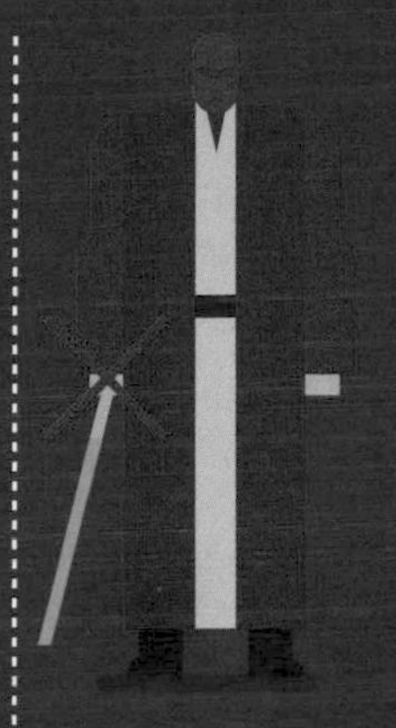

Ep. III **MACE WINDU**

RIGHT HAND

by Anakin Skywalker

Ep. III **CLONE TROOPERS**

2 HEADS AND 1 RIGHT ARM

by Yoda

Ep. VI **DARTH VADER**

RIGHT HAND

by Luke Skywalker

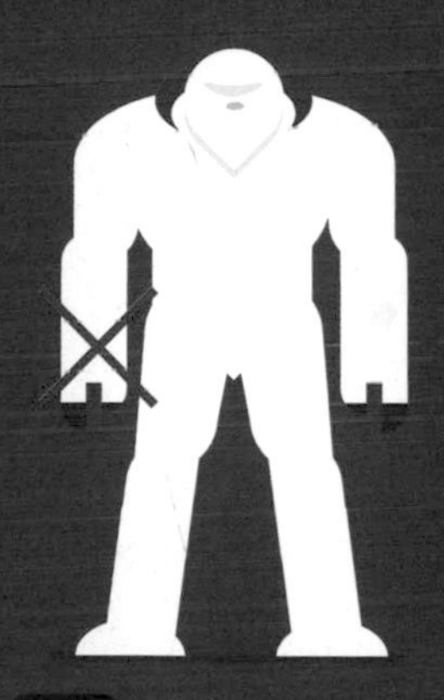

Ep. V **WAMPA**

RIGHT ARM

by Luke Skywalker

Ep. V **LUKE SKYWALKER**

RIGHT HAND

by Darth Vader

Ep. II

Ep. III

ANAKIN SKYWALKER

RIGHT FOREARM

by Count Dooku

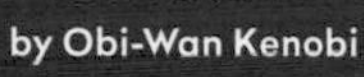

LEGS AND LEFT FOREARM

by Obi-Wan Kenobi

A LONG TIME AGO IN A GALAXY FAR, FAR AWAY, THERE WAS A PHRASE, A TITLE AND A FEW INTRODUCTIONS.

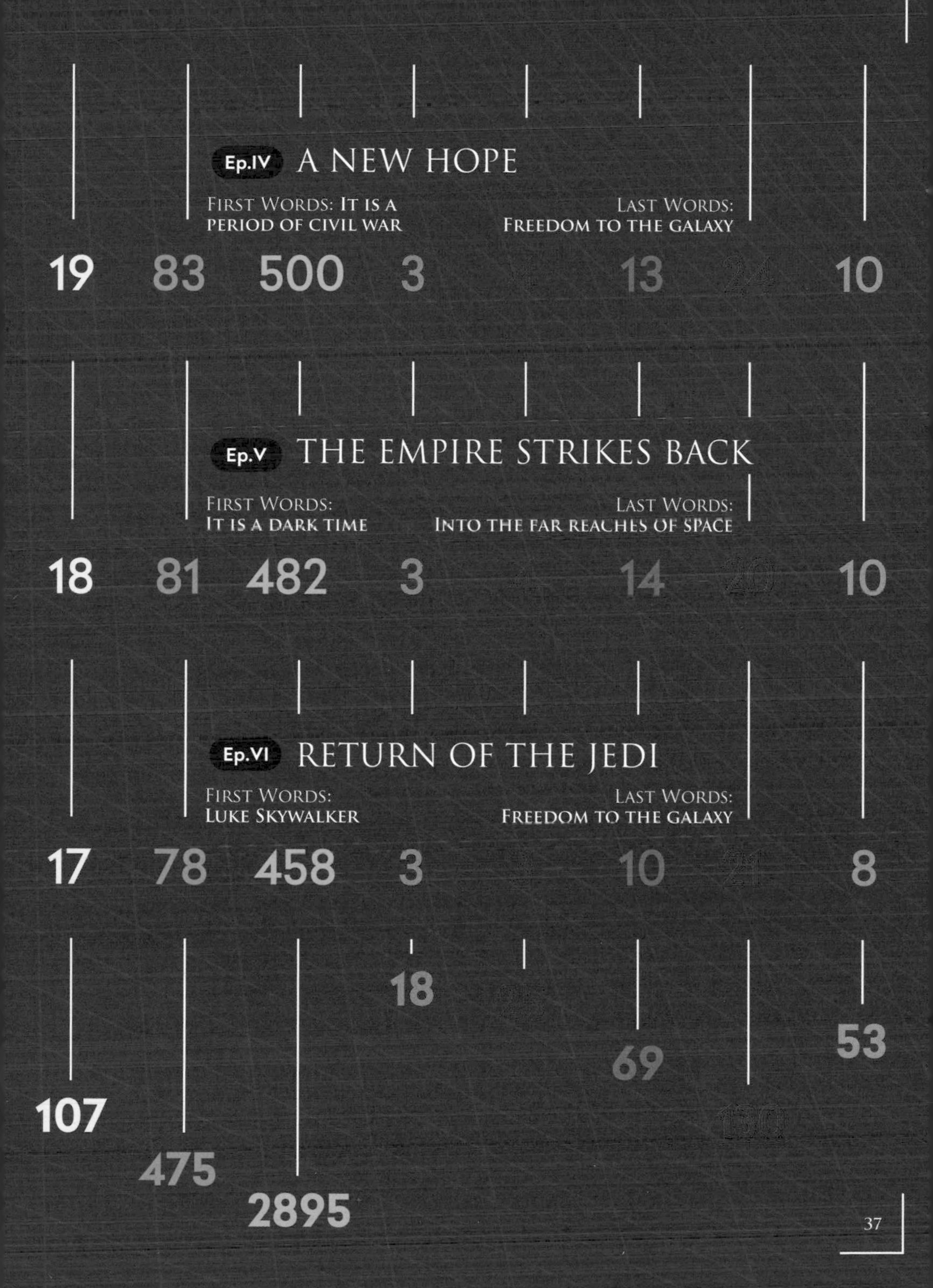
Ep.IV A NEW HOPE
First Words: It is a period of civil war
Last Words: Freedom to the galaxy
19
83
500
3
13
24
10
Ep.V THE EMPIRE STRIKES BACK
First Words: It is a dark time
Last Words: Into the far reaches of space
18
81
482
3
14
20
10
Ep.VI RETURN OF THE JEDI
First Words: Luke Skywalker
Last Words: Freedom to the galaxy
17
78
458
3
10
21
8
107
475
2895
18
69
53

A BRIEF HISTORY OF TIME

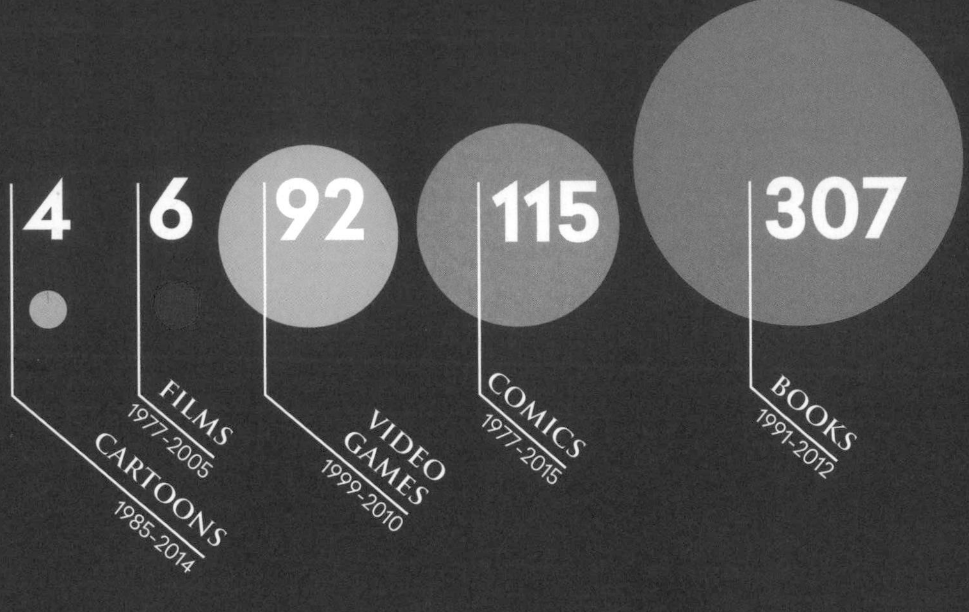

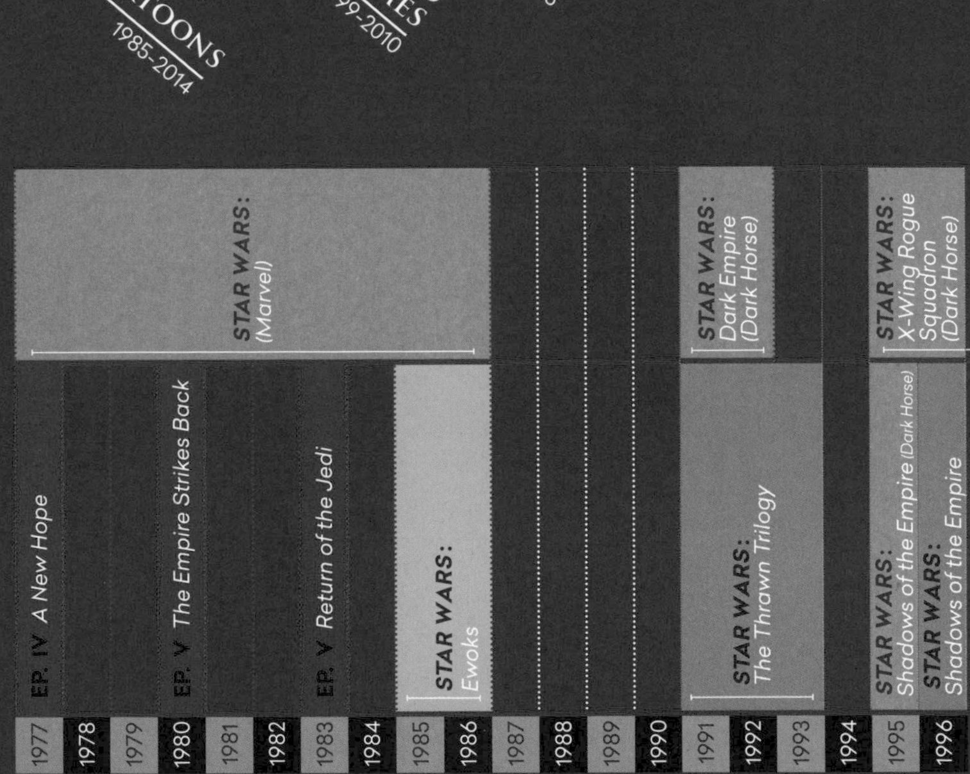

1997	**STAR WARS:** *The Han Solo Trilogy*	**STAR WARS:** *X-Wing Rogue Squadron (Dark Horse)*		
1998				
1999	**EP. I** *The Phantom Menace*	**STAR WARS:** *Episode I : Racer*		
2000				
2001	**STAR WARS:** *Tag & Bink are Dead (Dark Horse)*		**STAR WARS:** *Rogue Squadron II: Rogue Leader*	
2002	**EP. II** *Attack of the Clones*			
2003	**STAR WARS:** *Galaxies*	**STAR WARS:** *The Clone wars*	**STAR WARS:** *Knights of the Old Republic*	
2004				**STAR WARS:** *Knights of the Old Republic II*
2005	**EP. III** *Revenge of the Sith*		**STAR WARS:** *Lego Star Wars : The Video Game*	**STAR WARS:** *Labyrinth of Evil*
2006				
2007				
2008			**STAR WARS:** *The Force Unleashed*	
2009	**STAR WARS:** *The Clone Wars*			
2010			**STAR WARS:** *The Force Unleashed II*	
2011				
2012		**STAR WARS:** *Darth Plagueis*		
2013				
2014		**STAR WARS:** *Rebels*		
2015	**STAR WARS:** *(Marvel)*			

TRILOGIES I & II

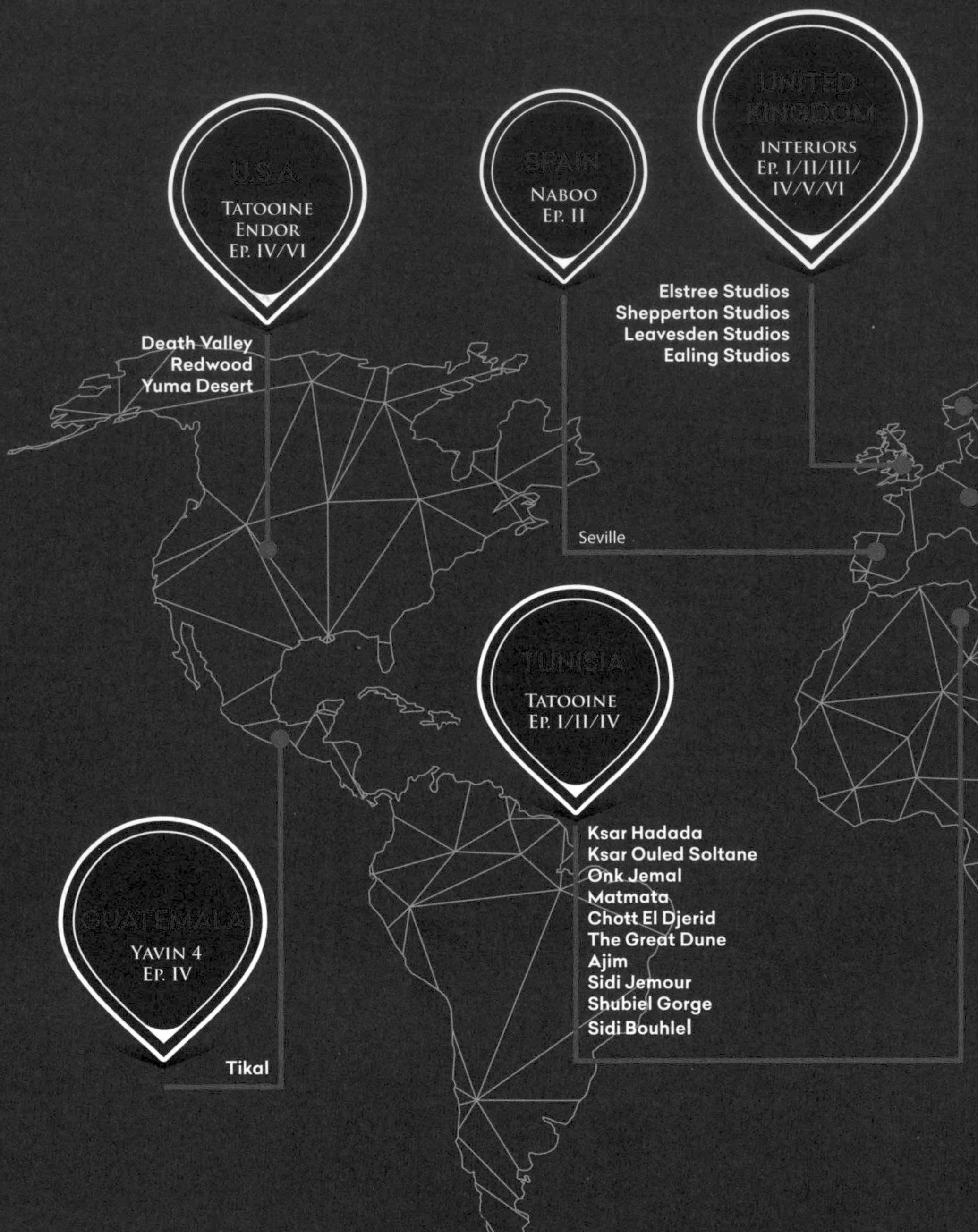

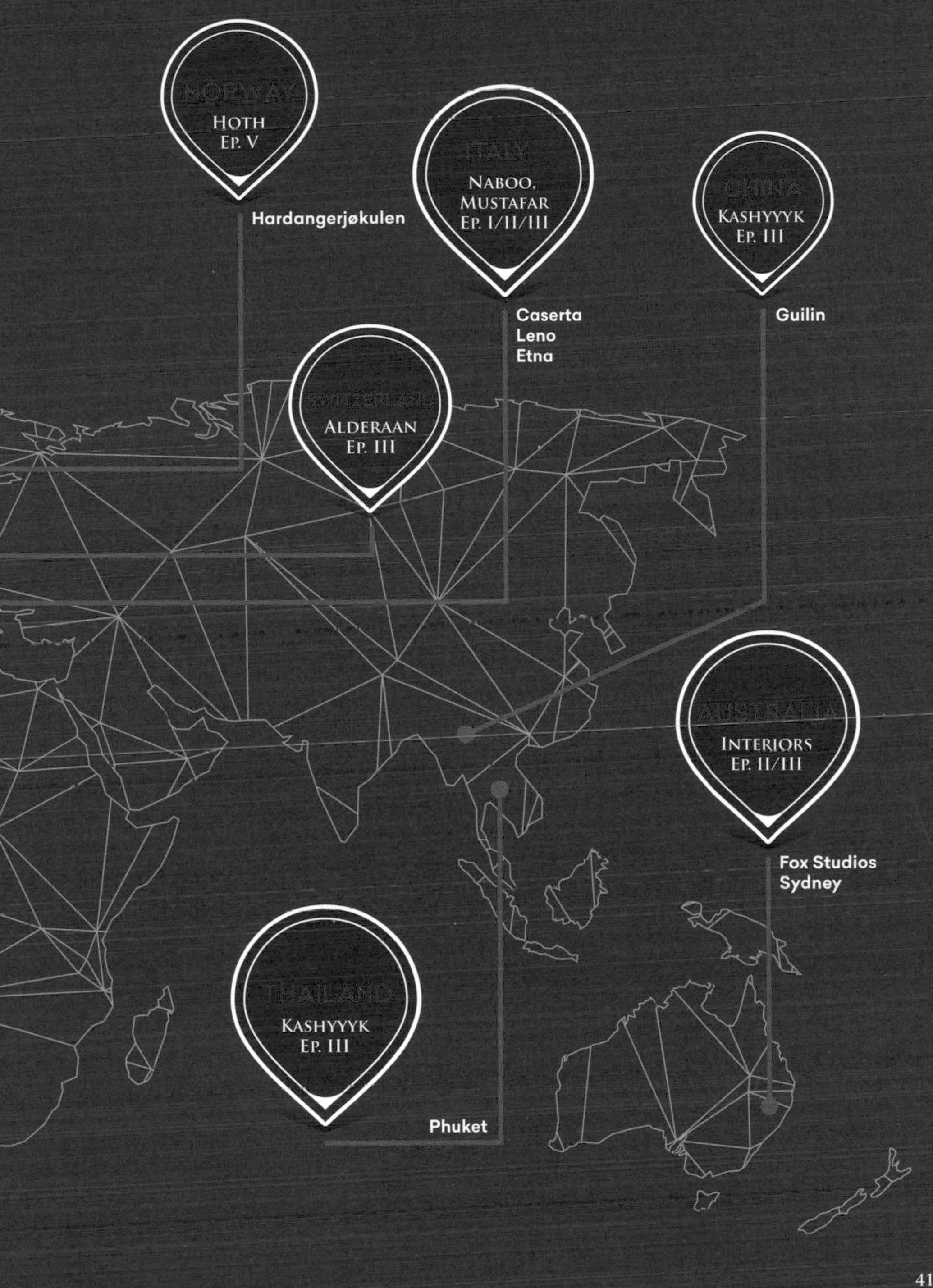

NORWAY
HOTH
EP. V
Hardangerjøkulen
ITALY
NABOO,
MUSTAFAR
EP. I/II/III
Caserta
Leno
Etna
CHINA
KASHYYYK
EP. III
Guilin
ALDERAAN
EP. III
AUSTRALIA
INTERIORS
EP. II/III
Fox Studios
Sydney
THAILAND
KASHYYYK
EP. III
Phuket

IT ONLY TOOK A FEW LINES FOR BOBA FETT TO BECOME ONE OF THE MOST POPULAR CHARACTERS IN THE GALAXY. AND THE REST?

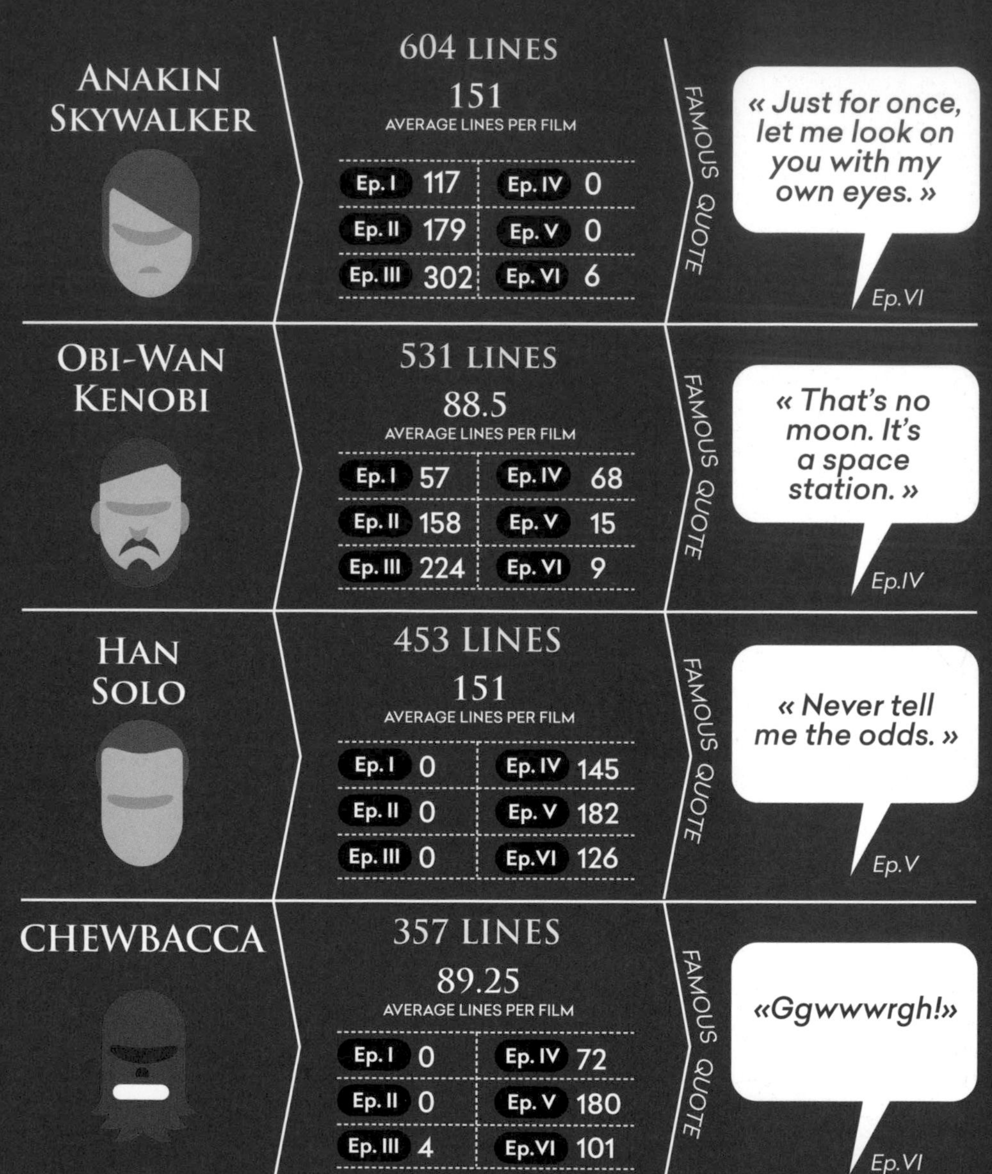

R2-D2

249 LINES

41.5
AVERAGE LINES PER FILM

Ep. I	46	Ep. IV	62
Ep. II	17	Ep. V	55
Ep. III	36	Ep. VI	33

FAMOUS QUOTE

« Beep chirp boop whistle. »
Ep.V

YODA

168 LINES

33.6
AVERAGE LINES PER FILM

Ep. I	18	Ep. IV	58
Ep. II	26	Ep. V	13
Ep. III	53	Ep. VI	0

FAMOUS QUOTE

« Do, or do not. There is no try. »
Ep.V

DARTH VADER

146 LINES

36.5
AVERAGE LINES PER FILM

Ep. I	0	Ep. IV	44
Ep. II	0	Ep. V	5§
Ep. III	6	Ep. VI	40

FAMOUS QUOTE

« I am your father. »
Ep.V

JAR JAR BINKS

101 LINES

33.6
AVERAGE LINES PER FILM

Ep. I	87	Ep. IV	0
Ep. II	12	Ep. V	0
Ep. III	2	Ep. VI	0

FAMOUS QUOTE

« Meesa cause mebbe one-a, two-y little bitty accidenties, huh? Yud say boom de gassa, den crashin deh boss's heyblibber, den banished. »
Ep.I

MACE WINDU

79 LINES

26.3
AVERAGE LINES PER FILM

Ep. I	13	Ep. IV	0
Ep. II	30	Ep. V	0
Ep. III	36	Ep. VI	0

FAMOUS QUOTE

« This party's over. »
Ep.II

HOW QUICKLY COULD YOU GET AROUND THE WORLD IN THE *MILLENNIUM FALCON* IF THE HYPERDRIVE WAS BROKEN?

366 H

38.1 H

17.6 H

9.2 H

5.5 H

4 H

48 MIN

2 MIN

LONDON-MOON

AROUND THE WORLD

LONDON-AUCKLAND

LONDON-TOKYO

LONDON-NEW YORK

LONDON-DELHI

LONDON-ORKNEY

AROUND THE M-25

Characters with the Most Action Figures

Luke Skywalker

(1978–2014)

Obi-Wan Kenobi

(1978–2014)

Anakin Skywalker

(1985–2014)

Darth Vader

(1978–2014)

Han Solo

(1978–2014)

Leia Organa

(1978–2013)

R2-D2

(1978–2013)

Boba Fett

(1979–2014)

Yoda

(1980–2014)

Darth Maul

(1999–2014)

Palpatine

32

(1984–2014)

Chewbacca

(1978–2014)

Stormtrooper

(1978–2014)

C-3PO

(1978–2014)

Padmé Amidala

(1999–2013

Mace Windu

(1998–2013)

Lando Calrissian

(1980–2015)

Jawa

(1978 –2009)

Greedo

(1978–2014)

7

Jabba

(1983–2010)

7

Salacious Crumb

(1984–2010)

Year	Number
2010	280
2000	
1990	260
1980	75
1970	21

STAR WARS

STAR WARS

STAR WARS

STAR WARS

810

NUMBER OF FIGURES PRODUCED BY DECADE

Midichlorian count by character

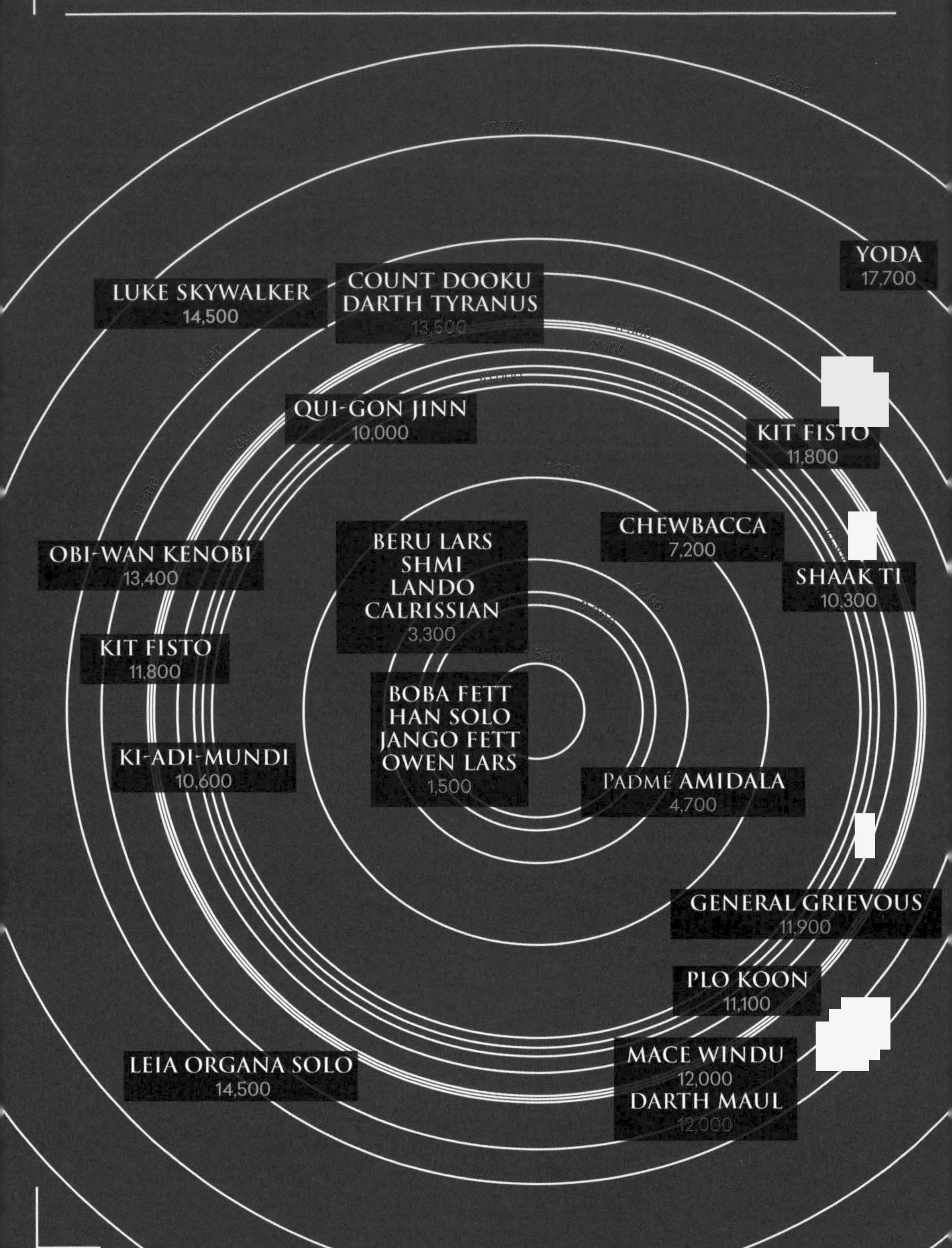

ANAKIN SKYWALKER
DARTH VADER
27,700

DARTH SIDIOUS
PALPATINE
20,500

MYTH OR REALITY?
THE DEBATE STILL RAGES
AMONG FANS, BUT ONE THING
IS SURE: IN THE *STAR WARS*
MYTHOLOGY, THEY'RE WELL
AND TRULY PRESENT.

AVERAGE COUNT FOR A JEDI:
10,000

MINIMUM REQUIRED TO
BECOME A JEDI: 7,000

JEDI

SITH

HUMANS

ANIMALS

MACHINE

AVERAGE MAN
L = 0.2m
W = 0.6m
H = 1.80m

74-Z SPEEDER-BIKE
L = 3m
W = 60cm
H = 60cm

B-WING
L = 16.9m
W = 2.9m
H = 2.5m (7.3m wings extended)

X-WING
L = 12.5m
W = 11.5m
H = 1.9m (2.6m wings extended)

TIE FIGHTER
L = 8.99m
W= 9m
H = 11m

SLAVE 1
L = 21.5m
W= 21.3m
H = 7.8m

JABBA'S BARGE
L = 30m
W= 9.8m
H = 5.3m

AT-AT
L = 20m
W = 5m
H = 22.5m

SANDCRAWLER
L = 36.8m
W = 10m
H = 20m

Y-WING
L = 16m
W = 7.9m
H = 2.9m

MILLENNIUM FALCON
L = 34.37m
W = 25.61m
H = 8.27m
(9.77m with legs)

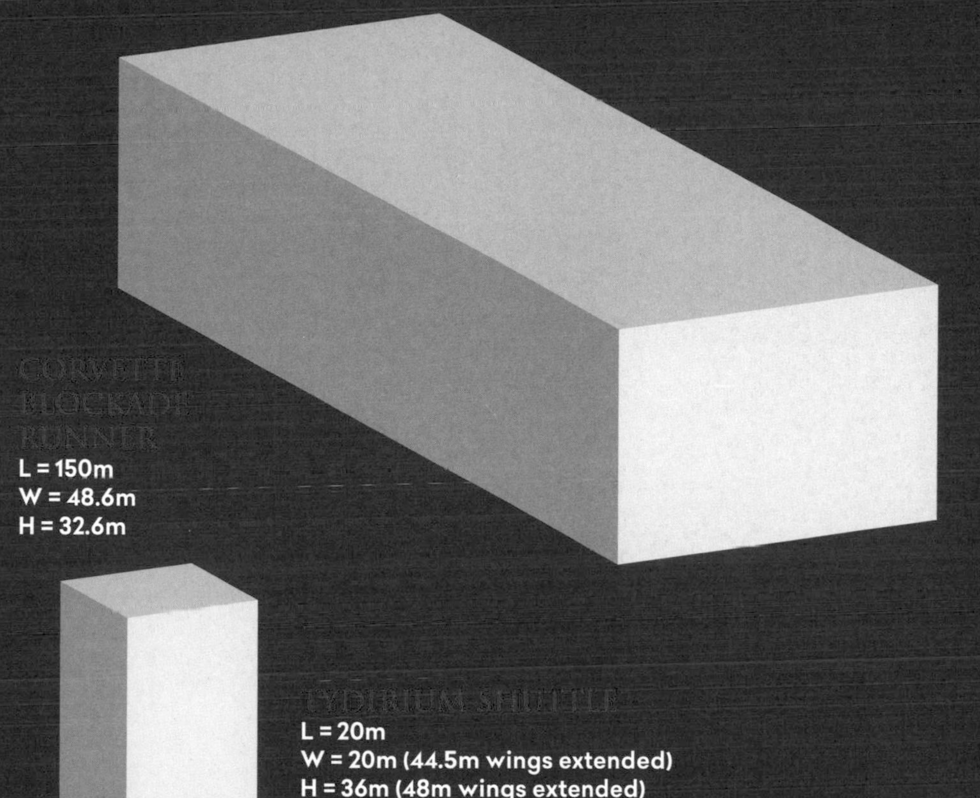

EXECUTOR-CLASS STAR DESTROYER

L = 19,000m
W = 11,000m
H = 6000m

20 YEARS LATER, HISTORY MIRRORS ITSELF, ... BUT NOT COMPLETELY.

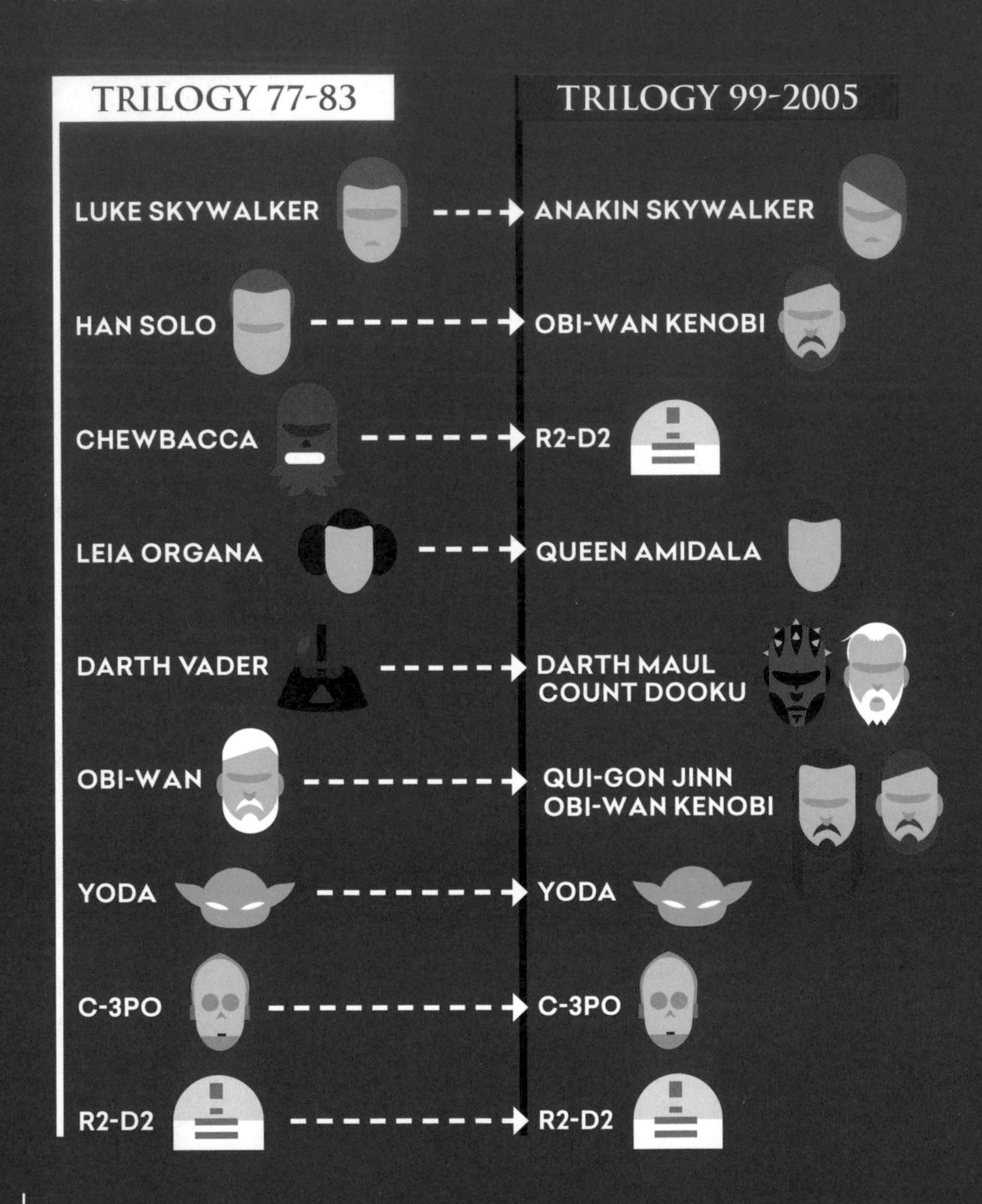

TRILOGY 77-83	TRILOGY 99-2005
PALPATINE	PALPATINE
STORMTROOPER	DROID ARMY
REBEL ARMY	CLONE ARMY
BOBA FETT	JANGO FETT
JABBA	JABBA
EWOKS	GUNGANS
WICKET	JAR JAR BINKS
DEATH STAR	VUUTUN PALAA

The *Imperial March* is a classic theme forever associated with Star Wars in the collective unconscious. It remains the central piece of John Williams' score which is as consistent as it is seminal.

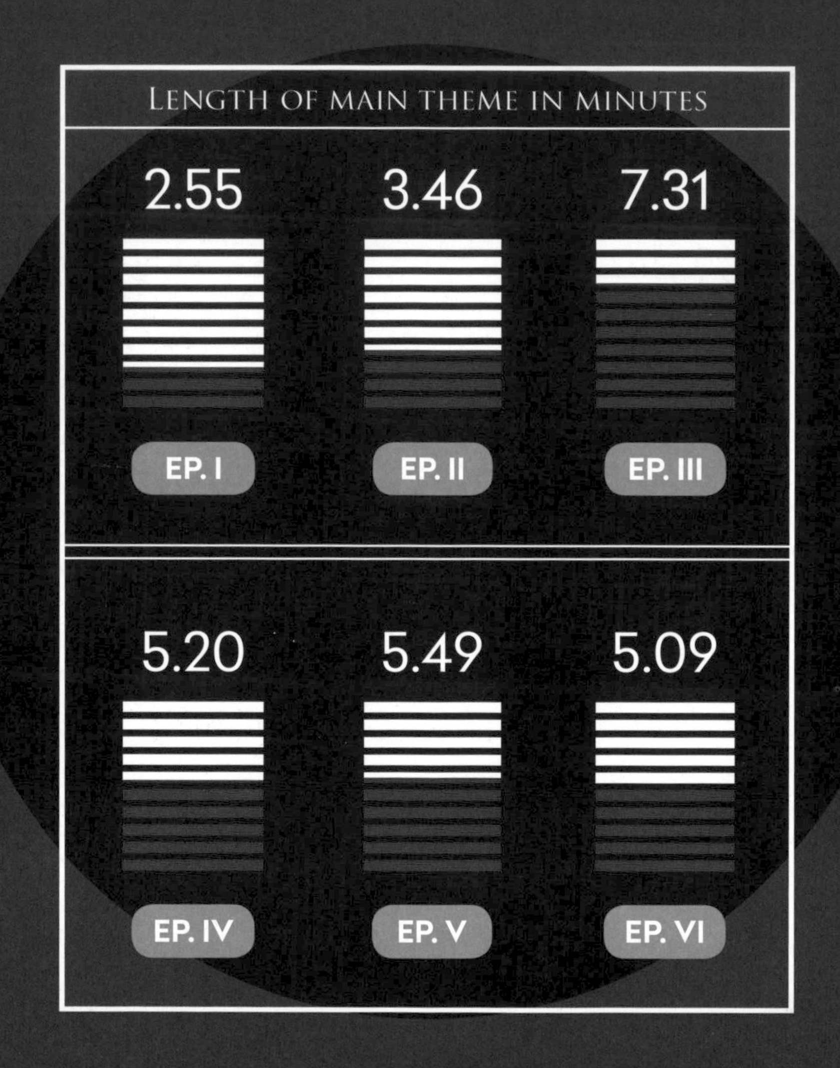

The Phantom Menace

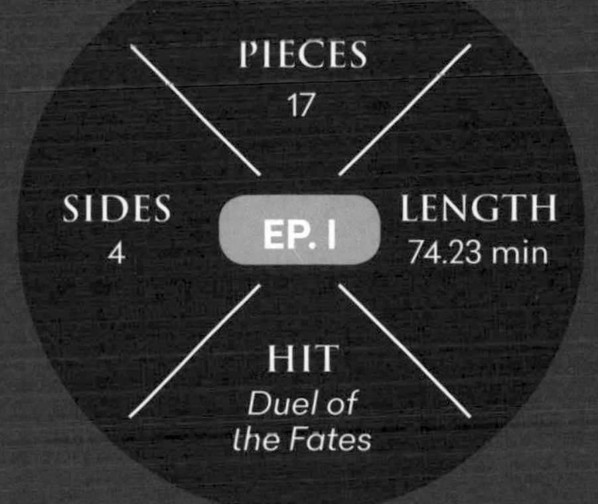

Attack of the Clones

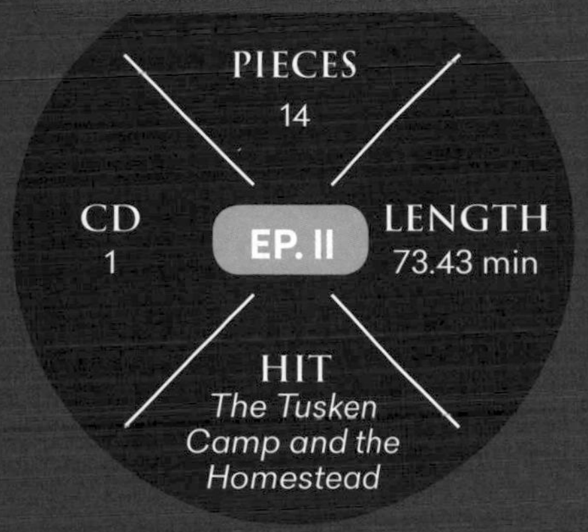

Revenge of the Sith

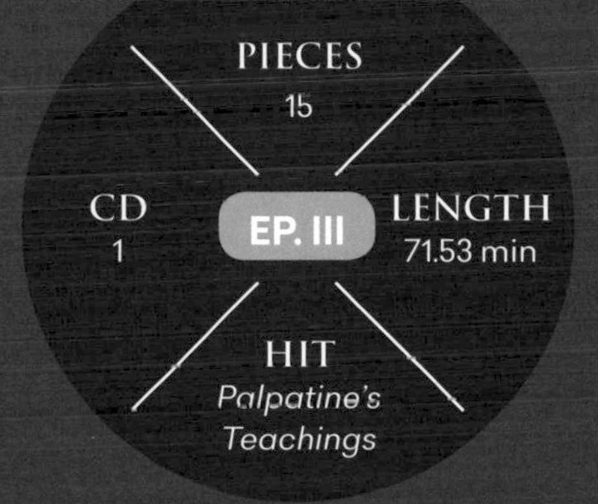

A New Hope

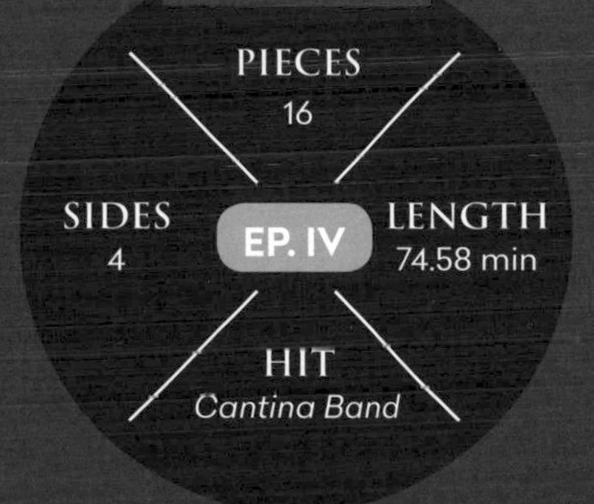

The Empire Strikes Back

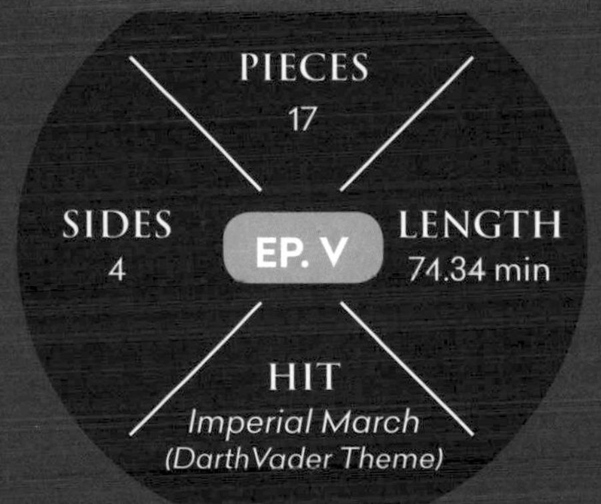

Return of the Jedi

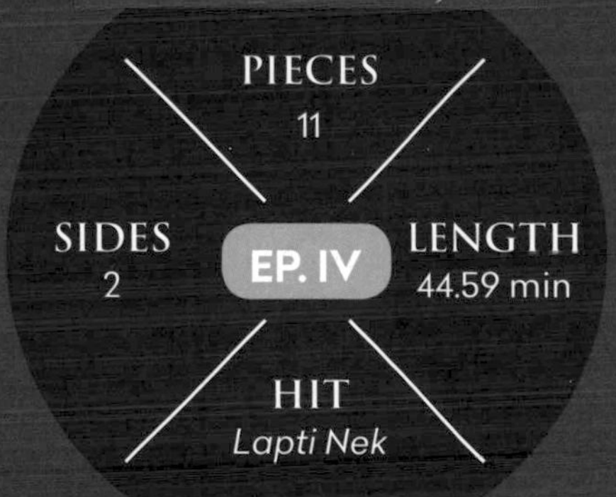

FIRST TRILOGY

[1977-1983]

CHARACTER HEIGHT

RANCOR
5M

CHEWBACCA
2.28M

DARTH VADER
2.02M

ABBA THE HUTT
1.73M

THE EMPEROR
1.73M

LANDO
CALRISSIAN
1.78M

SALACIOUS CRUMB
70CM

JAWA
1M

EWOK
80CM

MILLENNIUM FALCON

DIMENSIONS			SPEED	WEIGHT
Height 34.37m	Length 25.61m	Depth 8.27m	1050 Km/h	100 tons

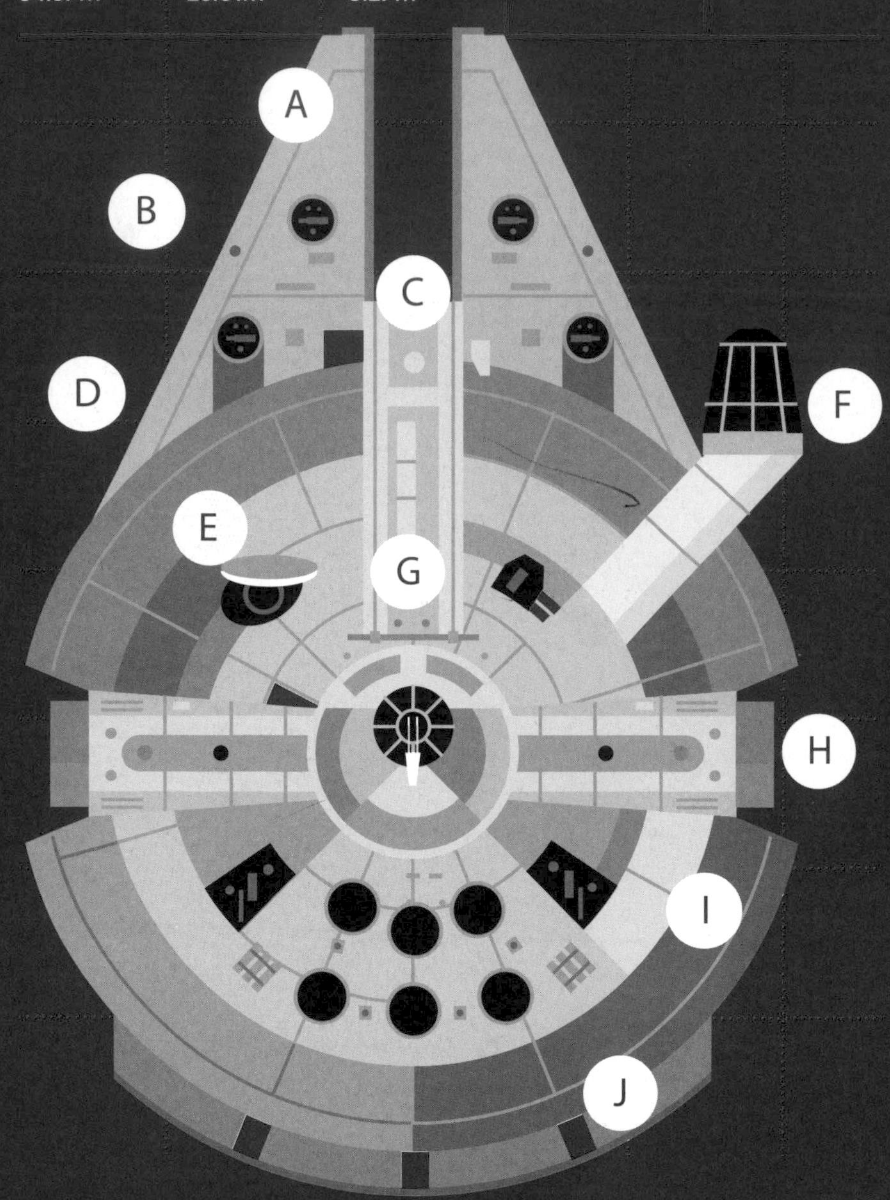

Range

1 AN 1 AN 1 AN 1 AN 1 AN 1 AN

Engines

2	Girodyne SRB42

Hyperdrive

Class 0.5

Weaponry

2	Corellian Engineering Corporation AG-2G quad laser cannons
1	AX-108 BlasTech “Ground Buzzer” blaster
2	Arakyd ST2 quad concussion missile launchers
1	Ganathan electric cannon
1	Mark VII tractor beam generator
/	Mines
/	Anti-missile propulsors

Shields

1	1 Torplex deflector shield generator
1	1 Novaldex shield generator
1	1 Kuat Drive Yards deflector shield generator
1	1 Nordoxicon-38 anti-concussion shield generator
1	1 deflector navigation system

Structure

A – Forward mooring mandible
B – Equipment access bay
C – Concussion missile launcher
D – Deflector shield generator
E – Tracking radar
F – Cockpit
G – Quadrilaser battery
H – Escape pod
I – Armour plate
J – Ion flux turbine

Small Craft

1 POD

Passengers

6

Crew Required

2

STAR DESTROYER

Imperial-I Class

Dimensions			Speed	Weight
Height 1600 m	Length 900 m	Depth 450 m	975 Km/h	36,000 tons

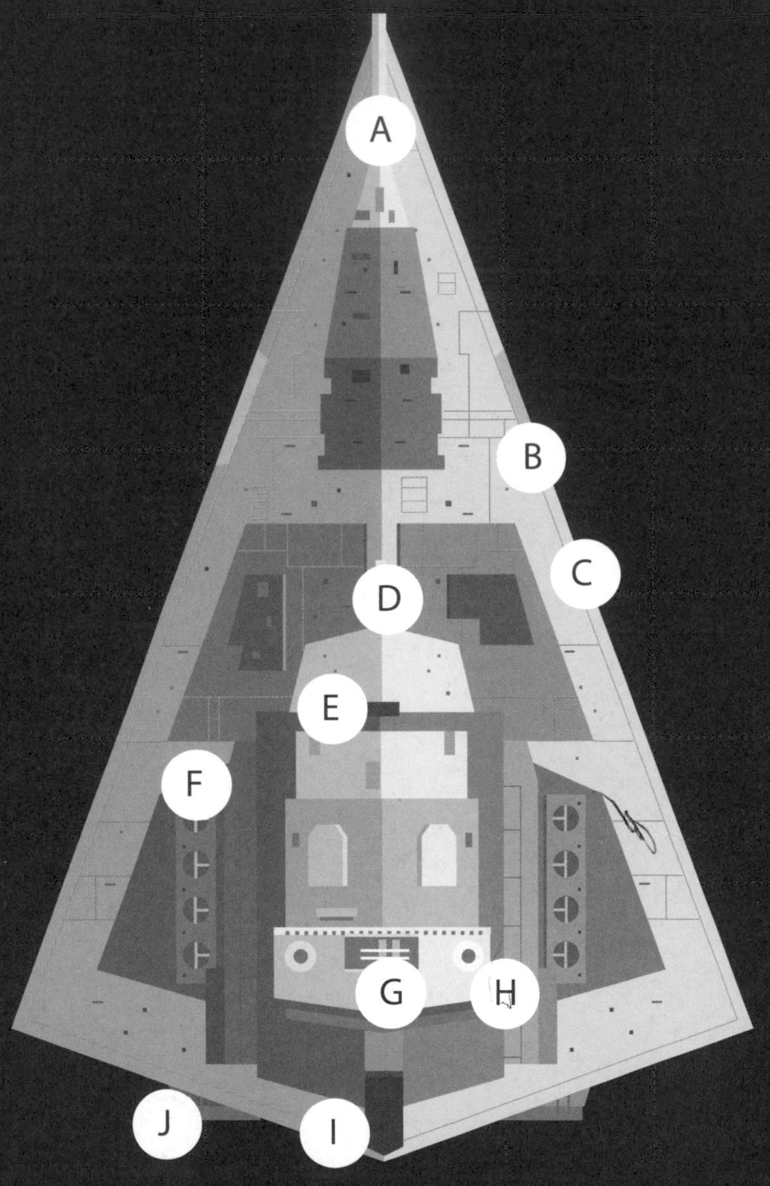

RANGE

1 AN 1 AN 1 AN 1 AN 1 AN 1 AN

ENGINES

3	DKY Destroyer-I ion engines
4	Cygnus Spaceworks Gemon-4

WEAPONRY

8	Octuple turbolasers or ion cannons
50	heavy turbolaser batteries
60	turbolaser batteries
26	supplementary turbolaser batteries (optional)
20	heavy ion cannons
10	Phylon Q7 tractor beam projectors

STRUCTURE

A – Computer-targeted turbolaser
B – Computer-targeted ion cannons
C – Computer-targeted turbolaser
D – Control room
E – Ion cannons
F – Turbolaser towers
G – Communication tower
H – Deflector shield generator dome
I – Solar ionisation reactor
J – Cygnus Spaceworks Germon 4

HYPERDRIVE

Class 2

SHIELDS

2	KDY ISD-72x deflector shield generator domes

SMALL CRAFT

72	TIE fighters
8	Lambda-class shuttles
8	Delta-class troop transports
5	assault shuttles
1	Gamma-class shuttle
20	AT-AT
30	AT-ST
/	Other vehicles

PASSENGERS

5000

CREW REQUIRED

9700

IN A GALAXY FAR, FAR AWAY

Death Star super laser

20 BILLION CREDITS

T-14 superspeed generator

20,000 CREDITS

Lightsaber **3000 CREDITS**

Stormtrooper's blaster

1000 CREDITS

SALE!

Chewbacca's bowcaster

FREE

Secret trip between Tatooine and Alderaan

17,000 CREDITS

HUSH-98 COMLINK

4000 CREDITS

GREEDO'S LIFE

4100 CREDITS

A DEATH STAR

1 TRILLION CREDITS

BLASTECH DL-44
(HAN SOLO'S BLASTER)

750 CREDITS

BRINGING SOMEONE BACK FOR A BOUNTY WITHOUT A WORK PERMIT

245 CREDITS

BOBA FETT'S DAILY EXPENSES

500 CREDITS

HIRE THE CANTINA BAND FOR A WEDDING (FIGRIN D'AN & THE MODAL NODES)

3000 CREDITS

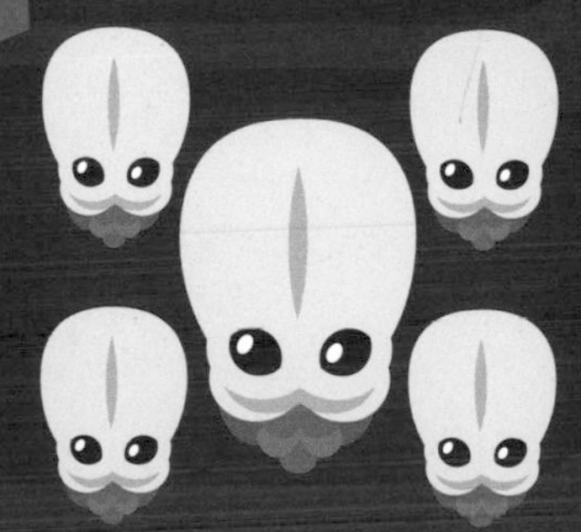

Episode IV - A New Hope

Character Journeys

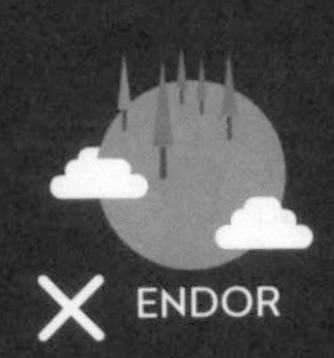

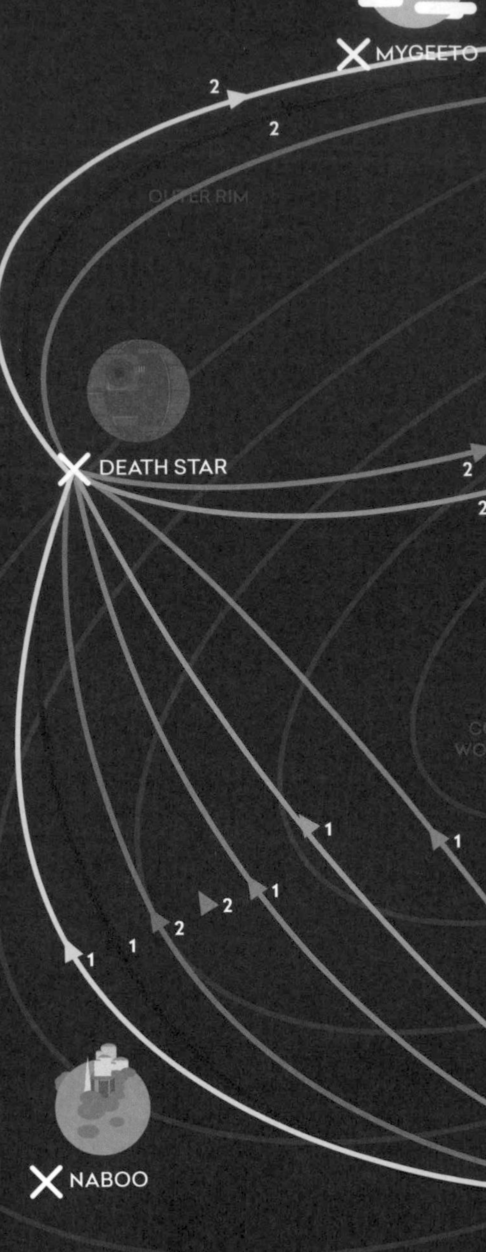

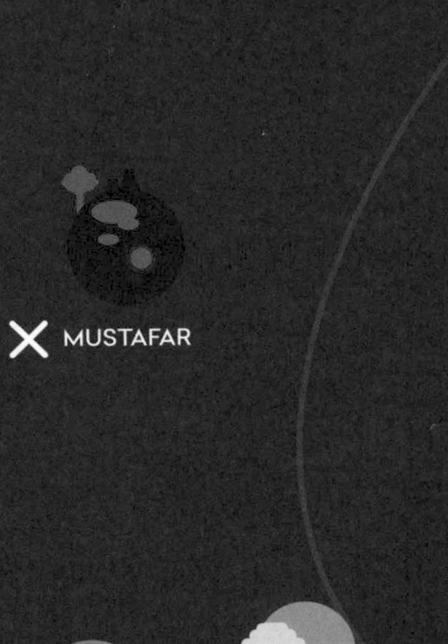

NABOO

DAGOBAH

UTAPAU

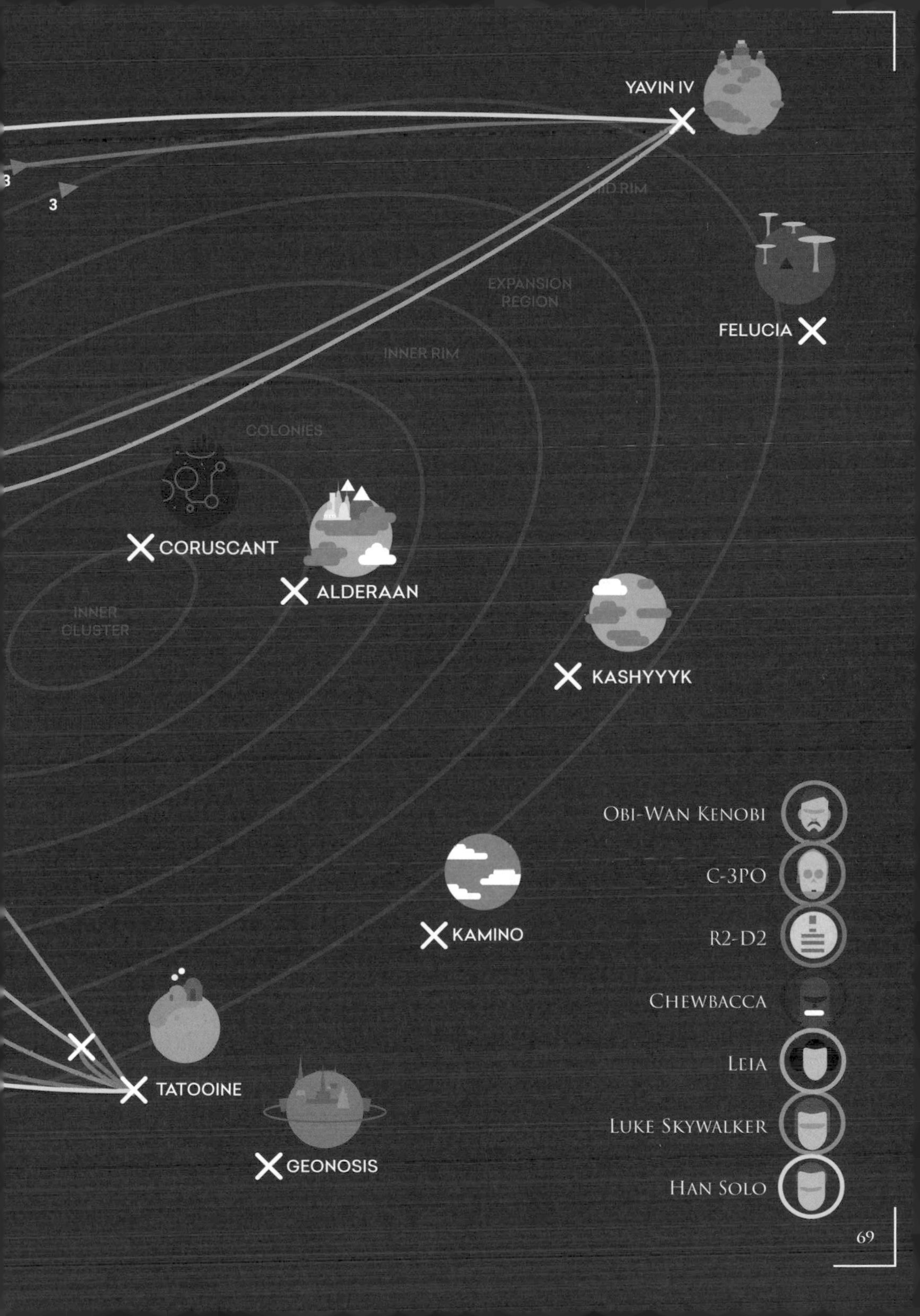
YAVIN IV
3
3
MID RIM
EXPANSION
REGION
FELUCIA
INNER RIM
COLONIES
CORUSCANT
ALDERAAN
INNER
CLUSTER
KASHYYYK
Obi-Wan Kenobi
C-3PO
KAMINO
R2-D2
Chewbacca
Leia
TATOOINE
Luke Skywalker
GEONOSIS
Han Solo

FINAL BATTLE

LOCATION : Space - Death Star

LENGTH/BEGINNING: 1:45:01 **END** : 1:57:16 = 12.15 minutes

WHAT'S AT STAKE: destruction of the Death Star

BEGINNING: lift-off of the rebel fleet on Yavin 4
END: Darth Vader escapes

FORCES PRESENT: 33 Rebel Alliance ships vs the Empire

KEY SHIPS

2 R-22 SPEARHEAD

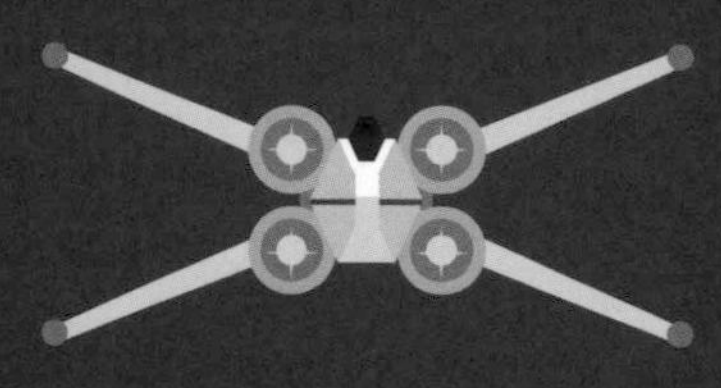

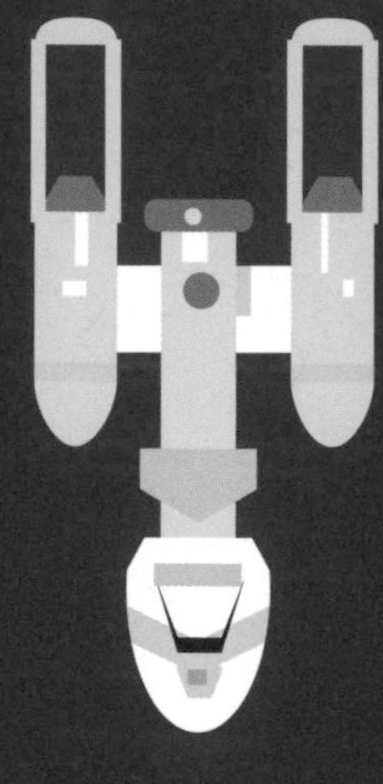

1 MILLENNIUM FALCON

VS

1 ADVANCED TIE

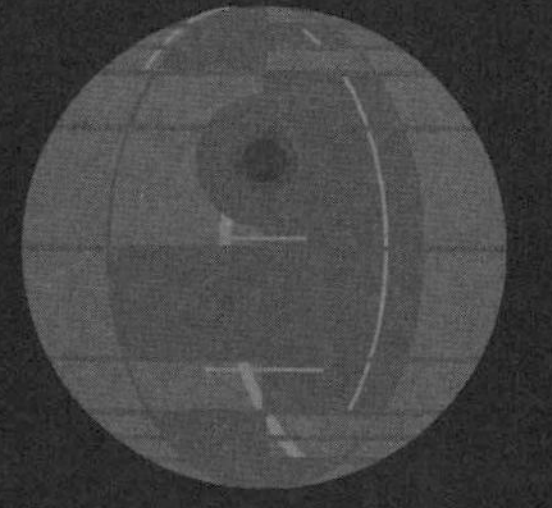

Commanders

Rebels

General Bob Hudsol | General Jan Dodonna | Princess Leia Organa

Empire

Darth Vader

Grand Moff Wilhuff Tarkin

Admiral Conan Antonio Motti

Grand General Cassio Tagge

Key characters

Rebels

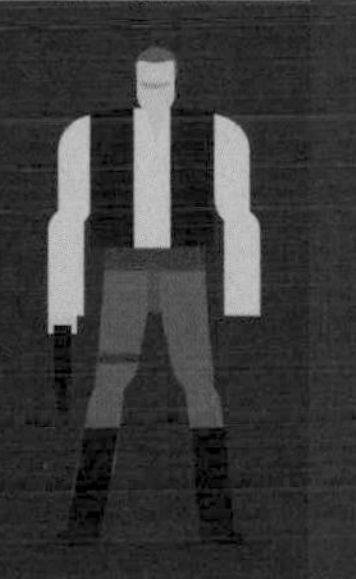

Han Solo

Empire

Darth Vader

Rebels

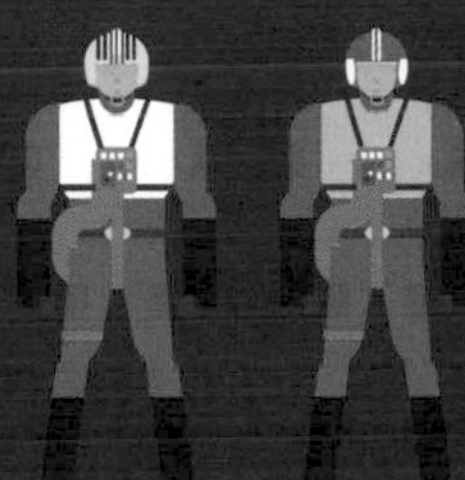

Garven Dreis (Red Leader)

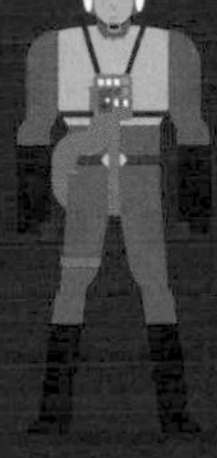

Wedge Antilles (Red 2)

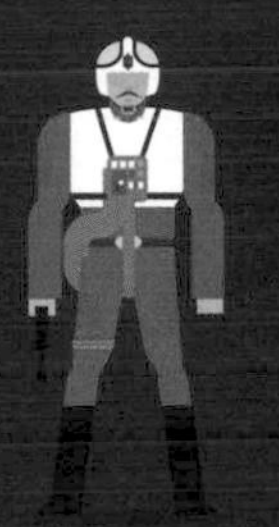

Biggs Darklighter (Red 3)

Tiree (Gold 2)

Rebels

Jek Tono Porkins (Red 6)

Theron Nett (Red 10)

Puck Naeco (Red 12)

Jon Vander (Gold Leader)

Luke Skywalker (Red 5)

Keyan Farlander (Gold 7)

Chronology and Events

Beginning: lift-off of the rebel fleet on Yavin 4

First strike: Biggs Darklighter
vs
turbolaser battery at 1.47.18

1st rebel loss: Red 6 at 1.47.29
(hit by the turbolaser battery explosion)

1st appearance of the Force:
Obi-Wan speaks to Luke at 1.47.40

1st X-wing destroyed by a TIE fighter at 1.48.11

1st feat of Wedge Antilles: destroys a TIE fighter at 1.49.21

1st incursion into the trench:
Gold Leader at 1.49.45

Luke, Biggs and Wedge enter the trench at 1.53.50

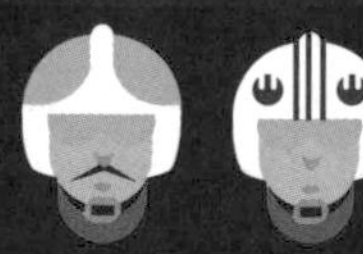

Obi-Wan speaks at 1.55.38

First shot: an ion cannon fired from the Death Star at 1.46.00

1st Empire loss: a stormtrooper on the Death Star (explosion of the turbolaser battery) at 1.47.19

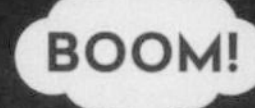

TIE fighters appear at 1.48.00

1st TIE fighter destroyed:
Luke at 1.48.31

Luke is hit at 1.48.5

TIE fighter destroys
1 X-wing (Red 12) at 1.52.41

Red Leader misses the target at 1.52.49

Wedge is hit at 1.54.36 and aborts

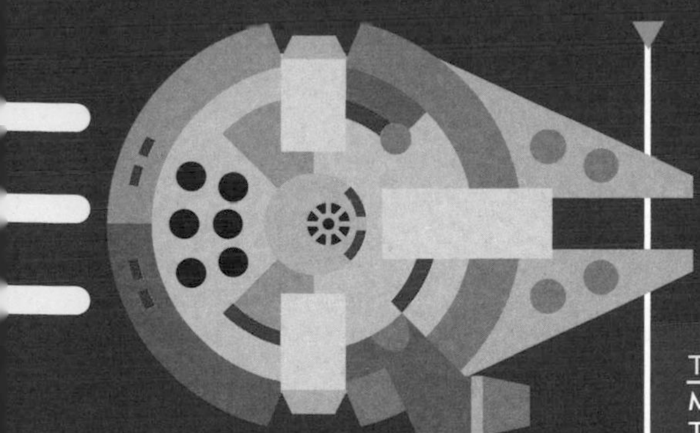

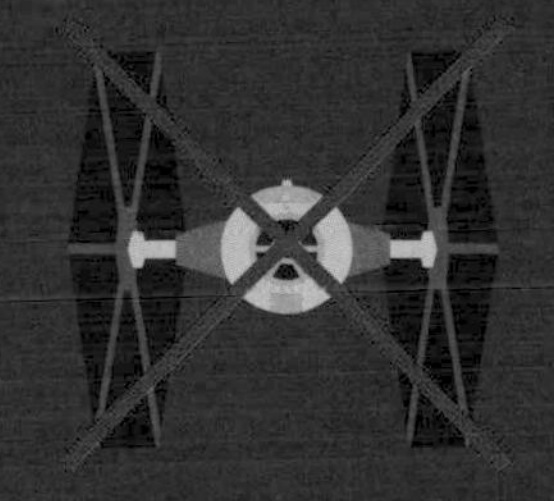

TURNING POINT

Millennium Falcon arrives, destroys a TIE fighter at 1.56.47

Torpedoes launched by Luke at 1.57.04

2 X-wings (Luke & Wedge),
1 Y-wing (Keyan Farlander),
and the *Millennium Falcon* escape.

The Death Star explodes at 1.57.16

Darth Vader escapes

In Brief

DARTH VADER'S SCORE

3 Y-WINGS
at 1.50.40 (Gold 2)
at 1.50.55 (Gold Leader)
at 1.51.03 (Gold 5)

2 X-WINGS
(Red 10) at 1.52.31
(Red Leader) at 1.53.19

Biggs Darklighter at 1.55.07
R2-D2 at 1.56.14

DEATH STAR

Dimension
120km diameter

Speed
10 MGLT

Lifespan
29 BBY–0 ABY

Cost
1,000,000,000 credits

Capacity
1 million kilotons

Structure
3 docking bays

12 Zones

A — superlaser focusing lens ("eye")

B — Equatorial trench

C — Polar trench

D — Meridian trench (north/south)

E — "Urban" surface blocks

F — Quadanium external hull

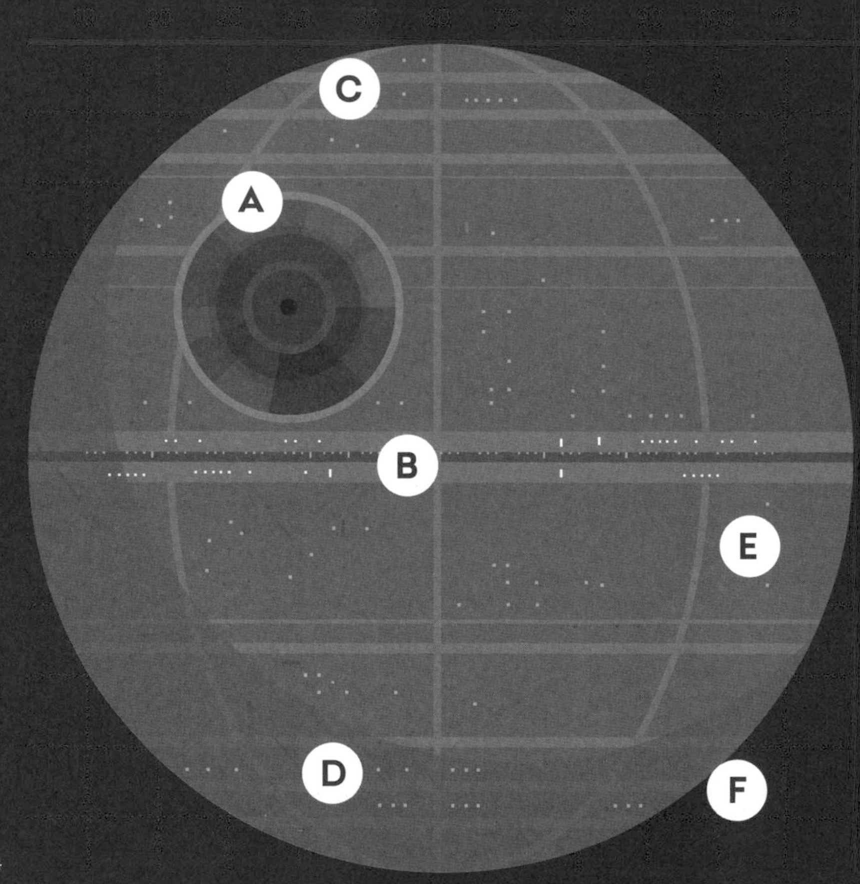

Range

1 AN 1 AN 1 AN 1 AN 1 AN 1 AN

Motor

1	motor

Hyperdrive

4.0 / 123 generators

Weaponry

1	Superlaser (range 47,060,000 km)
5,000	Taim & Bak D6 turbolaser batteries
5,000	Taim & Bak XX9 heavy turbolasers
2,500	SFS L-s 4.9 laser cannons
2,500	Borstel MS-1 ion cannons
	SB-920 laser cannons
768	Phylon tractor beam generators
	Particle blasters
	Magnetic machine guns
	Proton torpedoes
	Canons

Shields

2	KDY ISD-72x deflector shield generator domes

Small Craft

7000	TIE fighters
4	assault cruisers
3600	assault shuttles
1400	AT-AT
1400	AT-ST
1860	troop transports

Crew

342,953	regular crew		
27,048	officers		
607,360	troops including	25,984	stormtroopers
		57,278	gunners
167,216	pilots		
285,675	maintenance		
42,782	support staff		
843,342	passengers		
400,000	droids		

THE CANTINA

ADDRESS:
3112 Outer Kerner Way,
Mos Eisley, Tatooine

17	 TABLES
1	 BAR
58	 SEATS
102	MAX CAPACITY (HUMANS) AT THE MOMENT OF GREEDO'S MURDER
37	ALIENS
7	HUMANS
2	DROIDS

A – Cellar staircase

B – Office

C – Drink dispenser

D – Bar

E – Kiosk

F – Alcove table

G – Droid detector

H – Entry vestibule

I – Counter

J – Main door

K – Rear door

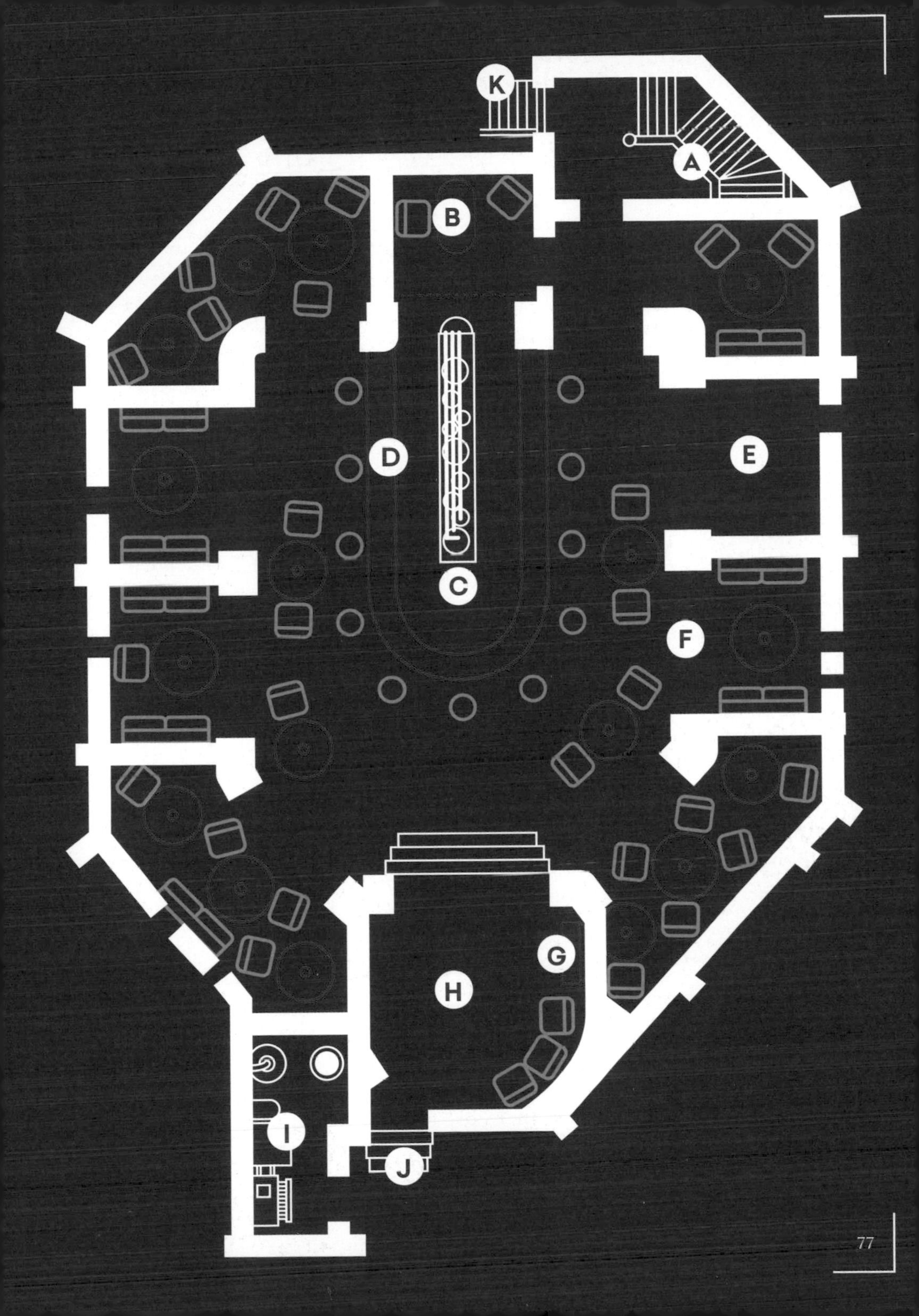
K
A
B
D
C
E
F
G
H
I
J

Character journeys

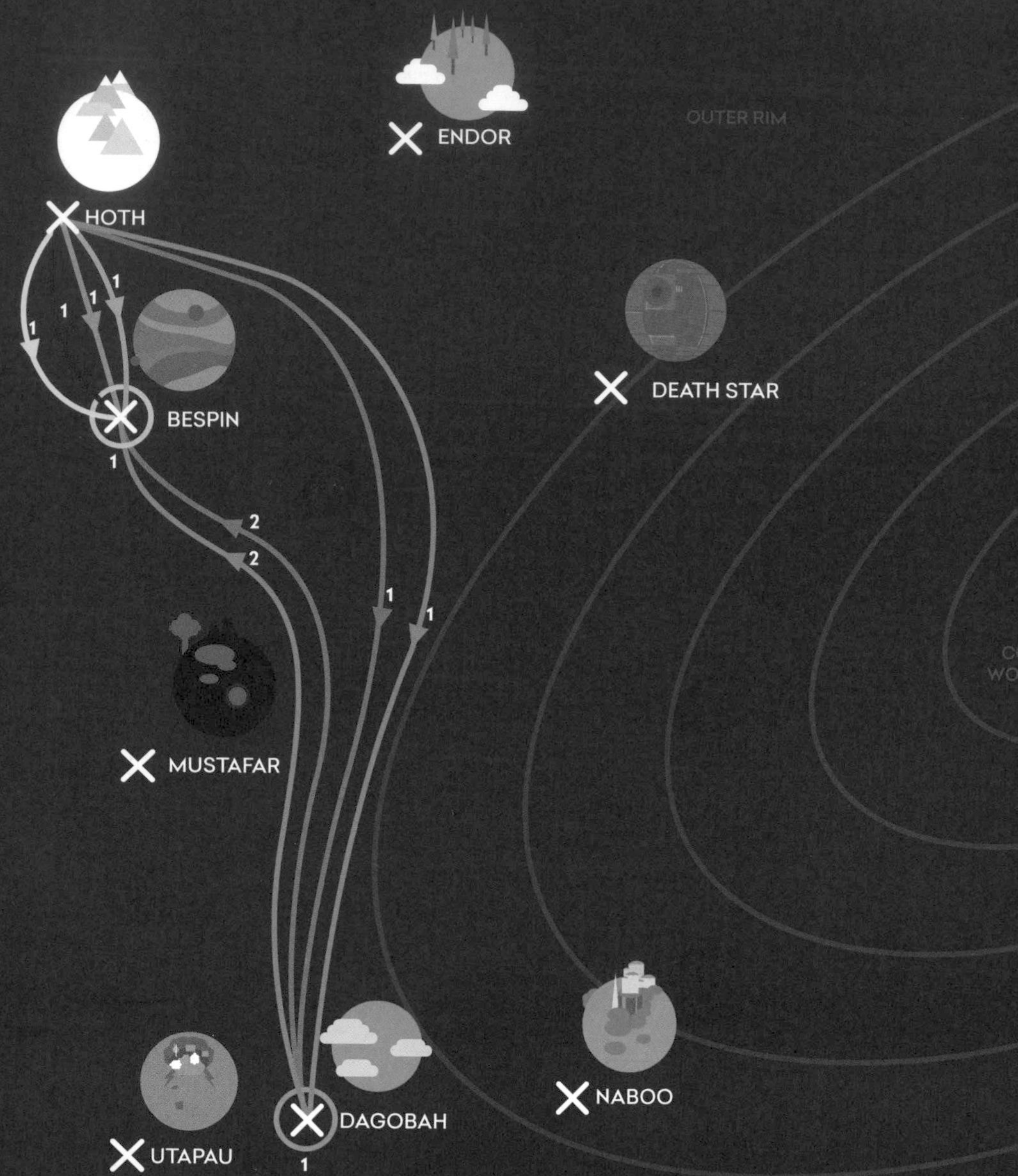

YAVIN 4

MID RIM

EXPANSION REGION

FELUCIA

INNER CLUSTER

COLONIES

CORUSCANT

1

ALDERAAN

INNER CLUSTER

KASHYYYK

C-3PO

R2-D2

YODA

PALPATINE

KAMINO

CHEWBACCA

BOBA FETT

TATOOINE

PRINCESS LEIA

LUKE SKYWALKER

GEONOSIS

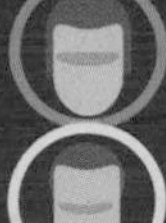

HAN SOLO

FINAL BATTLE

LOCATION : Cloud City - cryogenic chamber/landing bay

LENGTH/BEGINNING: 1.40.25 END : 1.52.13 = 11.48 minutes

WHAT'S AT STAKE: Luke vs Vader / Lando must escape from Cloud City

BEGINNING: a door closes on R2-D2

END: the *Millennium Falcon* launches

FORCES PRESENT: Jedi vs Sith/Lando Calrissian vs the Empire

KEY CHARACTERS

EMPIRE	REBELS					

DARTH VADER	LUKE SKYWALKER	PRINCESS LEIA ORGANA	LANDO CALRISSIAN	R2-D2	C-3PO	CHEWBACCA

1) CHRONOLOGY AND EVENTS: ON LEVEL 3

Vader's arrival at 1.40.48

Luke ignites his lightsaber at 1.41.06

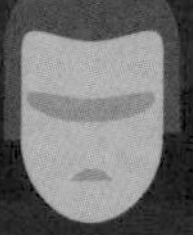

Vader ignites his at 1.41.09

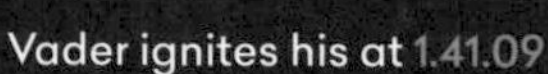

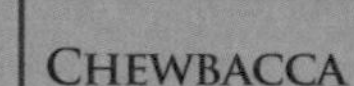

First clash at 1.41.17

Vader disarms Luke at 1.43.59

Luke escapes from the cryogenic chamber at 1.44.27

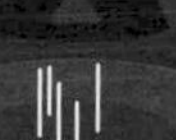

Luke falls into the cryogenic chamber at 1.44.22

"Impressive. Most impressive." Darth Vader at 1.44.37

Luke pushes Vader into the void at 1.45.13

Move to lower level at 1.45.38

Luke goes through the window at 1.46.42

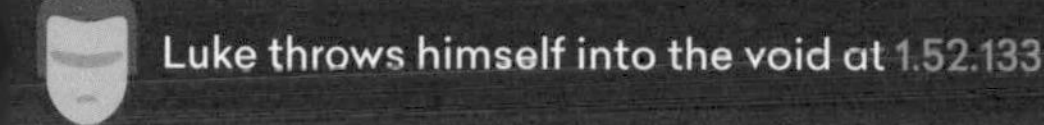

Move to the catwalk at 1.47.00

Vader cuts off Luke's hand at 1.50.26

Luke wounds Vader at 1.50.21

"I am your father." Darth Vader at 1.51.17

"Join me, and together we can rule the galaxy as father and son." Darth Vader at 1.51.52

Luke throws himself into the void at 1.52.133

2) Chronology and Events: on level 1

Cloud City Guards surround the stormtroopers at 1.41.50

Chewie strangles Lando at 1.42.15

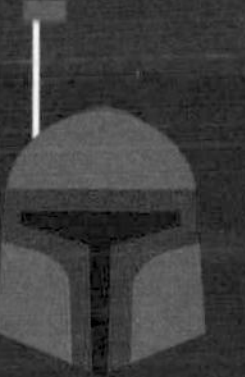

Boba Fett loads Han Solo in his carbonite at 1.42.55

R2-D2 joins the group at 1.43.08

Boba Fett escapes at 1.43.37

Lando evacuates Cloud City at 1.47.25

R2-D2 clears the security system at 1.48.22

The *Millennium Falcon* lifts at 1.49.21

Character journeys

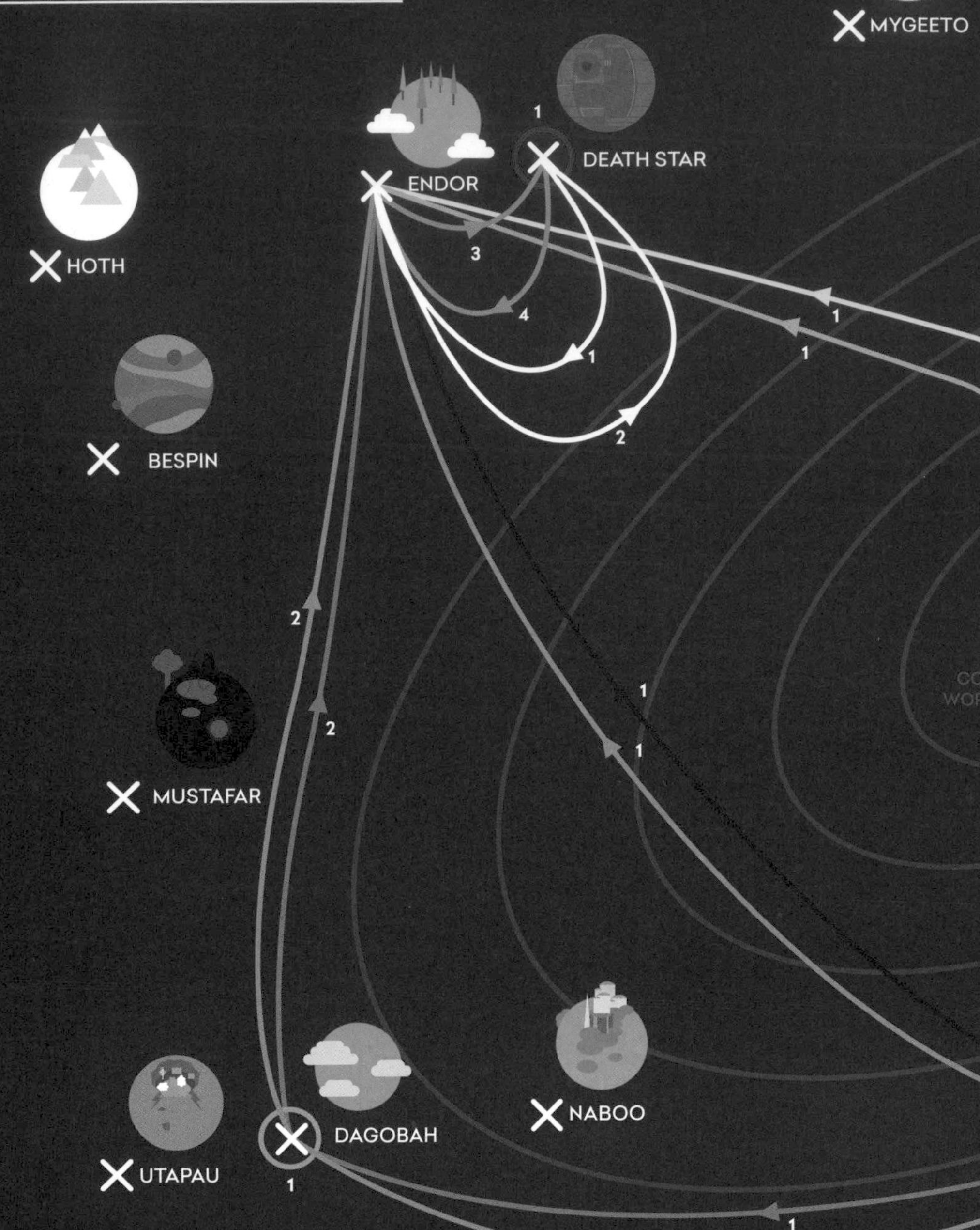

OUTER BORDER

YAVIN 4

MID RIM

EXPANSION REGION

FELUCIA

INNER RIM

COLONIES

CORUSCANT

ALDERAAN

INNER CLUSTER

KASHYYYK

KAMINO

TATOOINE

1

GEONOSIS

C-3PO 

R2-D2 

YODA 

PALPATINE 

CHEWBACCA 

BOBA FETT 

PRINCESS LEIA 

LUKE SKYWALKER 

DARTH VADER 

HAN SOLO 

FINAL BATTLE

LOCATIONS: Endor / Death Star / Space

LENGTH /BEGINNING: 1.28.51 END : 2.03.21 = 34.30 minutes

WHAT'S AT STAKE: deactivate the Death Star's shield, overthrow Palpatine and destroy the Death Star

FORCES PRESENT: Rebels & Ewoks vs Empire/Jedi vs Sith/Rebels vs Death Star

KEY CHARACTERS

REBELS

CHEWBACCA | HAN SOLO | PRINCESS LEIA ORGANA | R2-D2 | C-3PO | PAPLOO | WICKET

REBELS

LANDO CALRISSIAN | NIEN NUNB | WEDGE ANTILLES | ADMIRAL ACKBAR

JEDI

LUKE SKYWALKER

EMPIRE

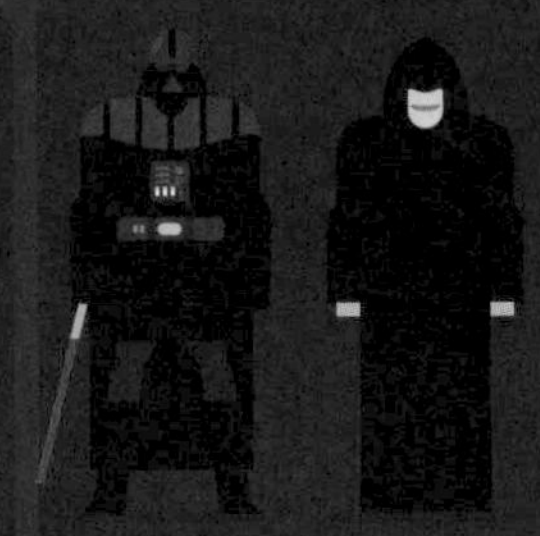

DARTH VADER | PALPATINE

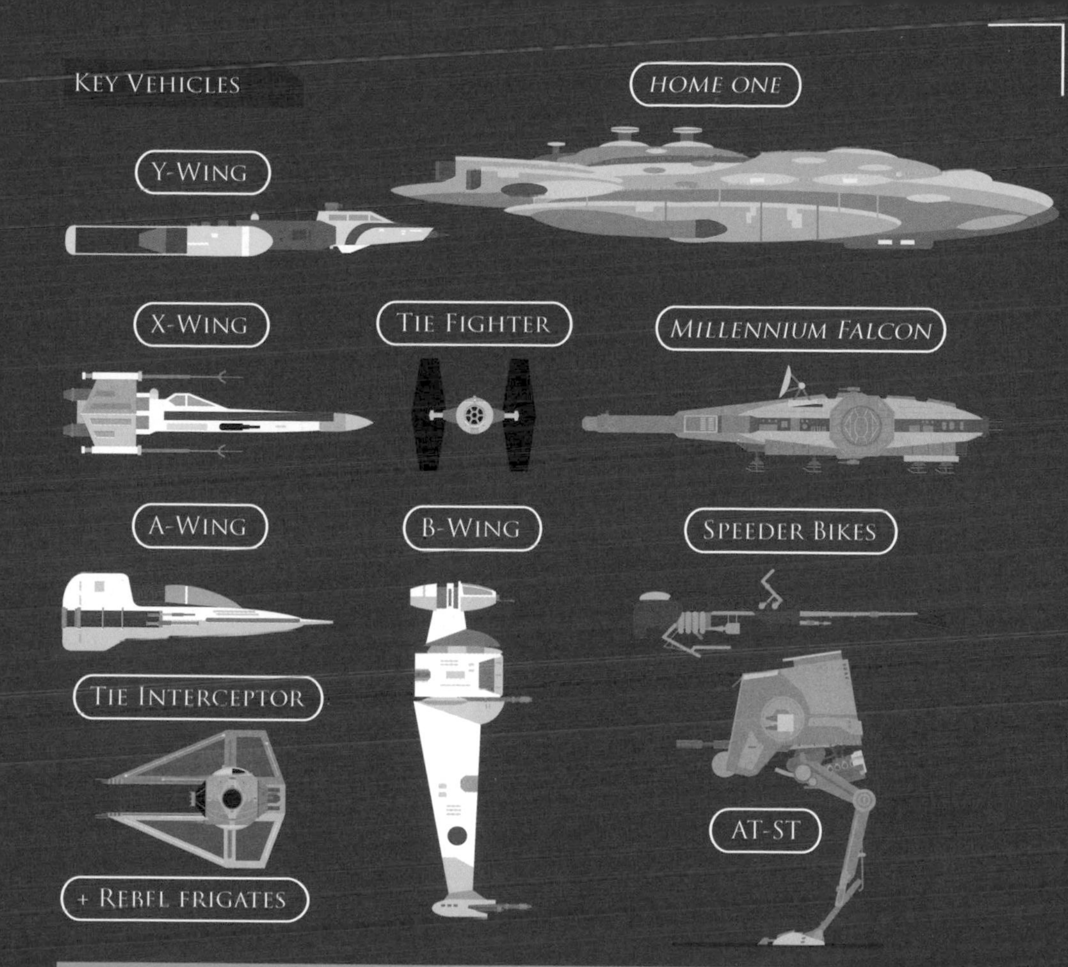

1) CHRONOLOGY AND EVENTS: BUNKER / ENDOR

4 scout troopers protect the bunker

Paploo steals the speeder bike at 1.28.51 pursued by 3 scout troopers

Paploo jumps off the speeder bike at 1.29.35

Last trooper arrested by the rebels at 1.29.44

Bunker opens at 1.29.48

Arrival in the control room at 1.33.20

Empire reaches the bunker at 1.33.40

Han, Leia, Chewie arrested. "You rebel scum" at 1.33.57

C-3PO distracts the Imperial troops at 1.37.11

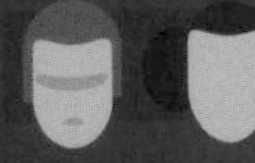

Han and Leia freed at 1.38.26

R2-D2 and C-3PO join Han and Leia at 1.42.47

2 Ewoks explode at 1.43.32. One dies.

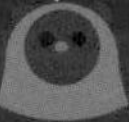

First AT-ST destroyed by Chewbacca at 1.46.30

Another at 1.47.19

Another at 1.47.46

Bunker sabotaged at 1.51.35

First Ewok attack on stormtroopers at 1.37.35

Wicket knocks himself out at 1.39.32

R2-D2 draws fire at 1.43.00

Chewbacca takes over an AT-ST at 1.46.19 / TURNING POINT

First vehicle destroyed by an Ewok: a speeder bike at 1.47.15

An AT-ST at 1.47.33

Leia is wounded at 1.47.55

Bunker explodes at 1.54.41

2) Chronology and Events:
Death Star

Luke surrenders to Darth Vader at 1.23.14

Darth Vader to Luke at 1.25.25
"It is too late for me, my son."

Vader's *Tydirium* lifts at 1.26.19

The Emperor tells Luke that he knows the rebels' plans at 1.32.10

Death Star fires for the first time at 1.41.55

Vader ignites his lightsaber at 1.45.22

Luke makes Vader fall at 1.48.50

Vader resumes the duel at 1.49.34

Vader discovers Leia's existence at 1.52.21

TURNING POINT

Luke strikes Vader down at 1.53.21

Luke turns away from the dark side at 1.54.09 "Never. I'll never turn to the dark side." – Luke to the Emperor

RETURN OF THE JEDI

Vader seizes the Emperor at 1.56.55

Luke meets the Emperor at 1.30.46

Luke witnesses the attack at 1.35.36

Luke retrieves his lightsaber at 1.45.22

First clash at 1.45.23

Luke stops fighting at 1.49.05

STOP

Vader officially wavers. "Your thoughts betray you, father." – Luke Skywalker to Darth Vader at 1.50.00. Interruption of duel.

Luke resumes the duel at 1.52.48

Luke cuts off Vader's hand at 1.53.24

The Emperor attacks Luke at 1.55.14

Destruction of the Emperor at 1.57.10

IN BRIEF

NUMBER OF LIGHTSABER CLASHES:
49 (green vs red)

3) CHRONOLOGY AND EVENTS:
SPACE / DEATH STAR

Lando engages lightspeed at 1.27.43

Millennium Falcon arrives within range of Death Star at 1.34.05

Lando sees the trap at 1.34.46

"It's a trap!" Admiral Ackbar at 1.35.09

Appearance of the Imperial Fleet at 1.35.11

First Imperial attack at 1.35.14

Death Star fires for the first time at 1.41.55

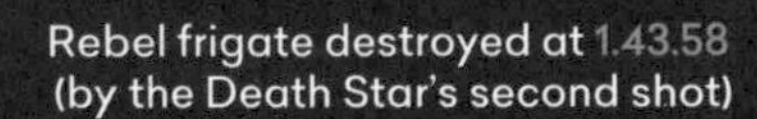

Rebel frigate destroyed at 1.41.58

Rebel frigate destroyed at 1.43.58 (by the Death Star's second shot)

Death Star's shield falls at 1.54.53
TURNING POINT

The *Millennium Falcon* enters the Death Star at 1.57.55

The *Millennium Falcon* loses its deflector shield at 1.58.39

Star Destroyer destroyed at 1.58.52

Super Star Destroyer destroyed at 1.59.30

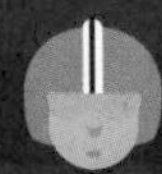

Wedge hits the bullseye at 2.02.15

The *Millennium Falcon* hits the bullseye at 2.02.22

Death Star II destroyed at 2.03.08

BOOM!

The *Millennium Falcon* gets away at 2.03.01

TIE destroyed

5 fighters
7 Interceptors
3 by the *Millennium Falcon*
Total = 12

Wings Destroyed

2 A-Wing
3 X-Wing
1 Y-Wing
Total = 6

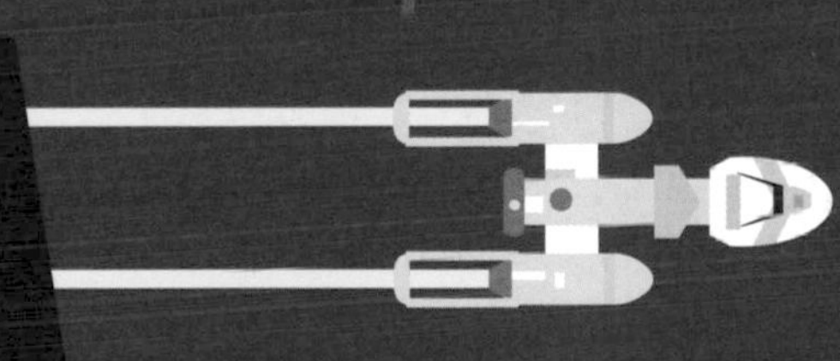

Dimension	Speed	Structure
160 km/diameter	20 MGLT	1 Docking bay
Life span		12 Zones
29 BBY–0 ABY		A — Superlaser focusing lens ("eye")
Cost		B — Equatorial trench
1,000,000,000 credits		C — North command sector
		D — South command sector
Capacity		E — Reactor core (internal)
1 million kilotons		F — Exposed superstructure

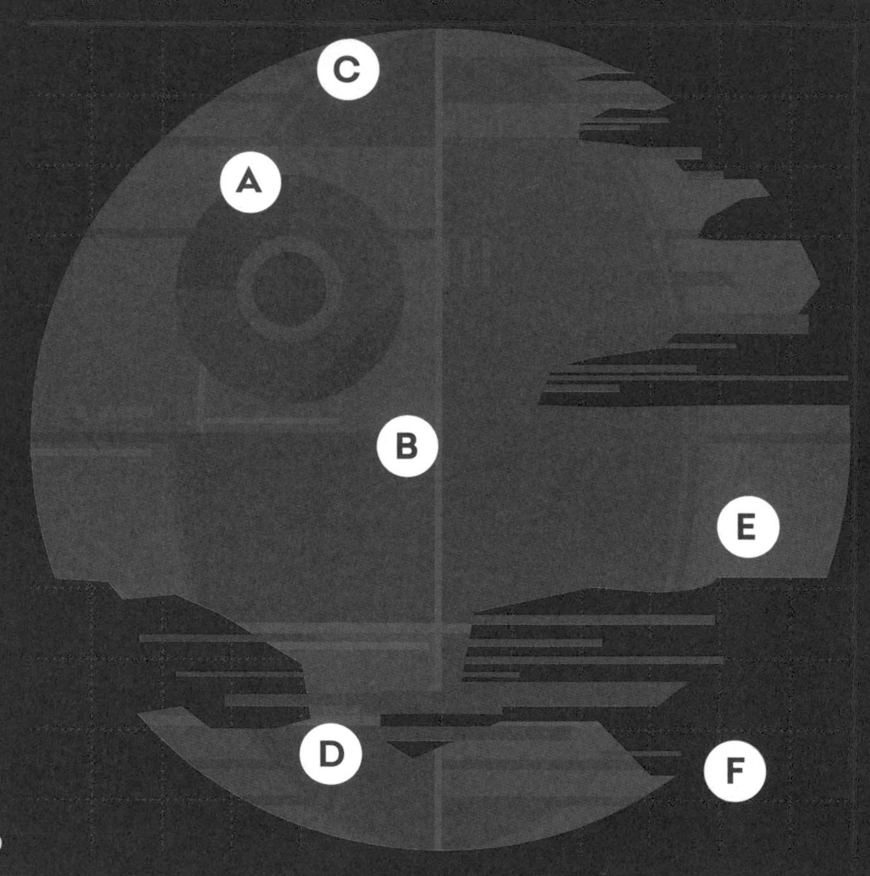

Range

1 AN | 1 AN | 1 AN | 1 AN | 1 AN | 1 AN

Motor

/	incomplete

Hyperdrive

3.0

Weaponry

1	Superlaser (range 47,060,000 km)
15,000	Taim & Bak D6 turbolaser batteries
15,000	Taim & Bak XX9 heavy turbolasers
7,500	SFS L-s 4.9 laser cannons
5,000	Borstel MS-1 ion cannons
768	Phylon tractor beam generators

Small Craft

7200	TIE fighters
16	Destroyers
3600	*Tydirium* shuttles
2480	Skipray patrol boats
1400	AT-AT
1400	AT-ST
1420	Repulsor tanks
1420	Repulsor craft
4843	HAVw A5 Juggernauts
178	PX-4 mobile bases
355	HAVr A9 flying fortresses
1860	Troop transports

Crew

485,560	Regular crew		
27,048	Officers		
1,295,950	Troops including	127,570	stormtroopers
		152,275	gunners
334,432	Pilots		
75,860	Maintenance		

TOTAL : 224,190 CREDITS

1 dumped cargo :	**12,400 credits**
1 dead employee (Greedo): :	**4100 credits**
Advances on the *Millennium Falcon*:	**125,640 credits**
Bounty notices:	**320 credits**
Boba Fett bounty:	**5000 credits** (500 /day)
Extra bounties:	**2000 credits** (50 credits /day/hunter)
Interest, 50%:	**74,730 credits**

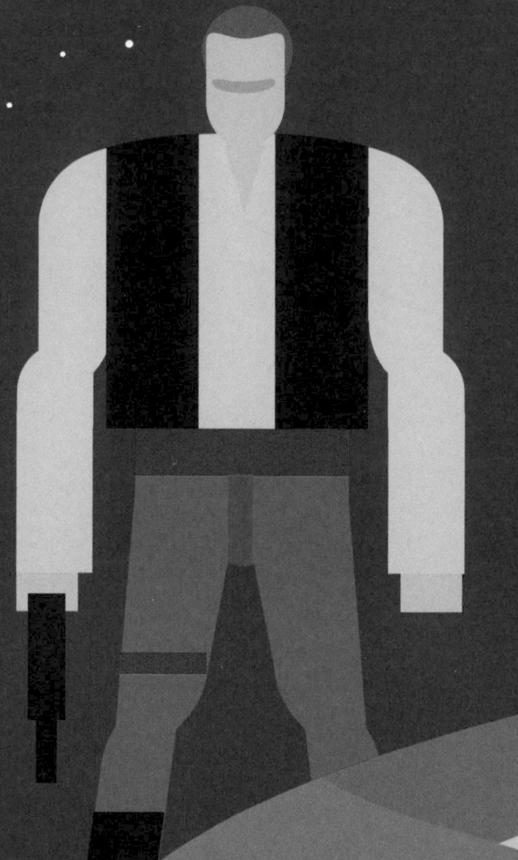

WHAT DOES A JEDI USE EACH ITEM FOR?

A GLOWROD
[flashlight]

A TOOLBOX
[for lightsaber repair]

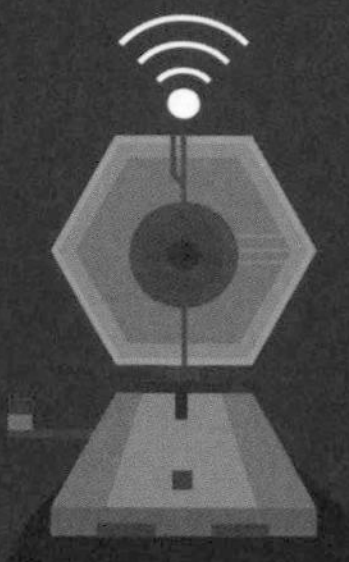

A TRANSCEIVER BEACON
[for communicating]

A GRAPPLING HOOK
[for climbing things]

A HUSH-98 COMLINK
[for communicating]

A HOLOPROJECTOR
[for communicating]

AN A99 AQUATA BREATHER
[for breathing underwater]

A LIGHTSABER
[for fighting]

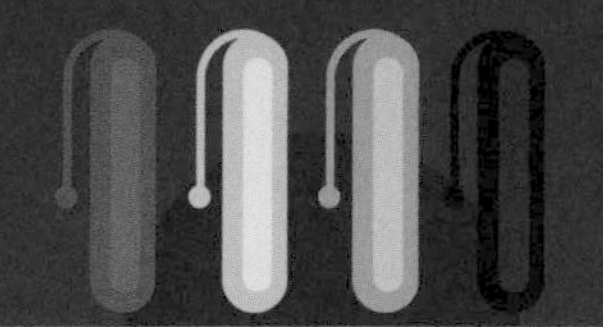

FOOD & ENERGY CAPSULES
[for eating]

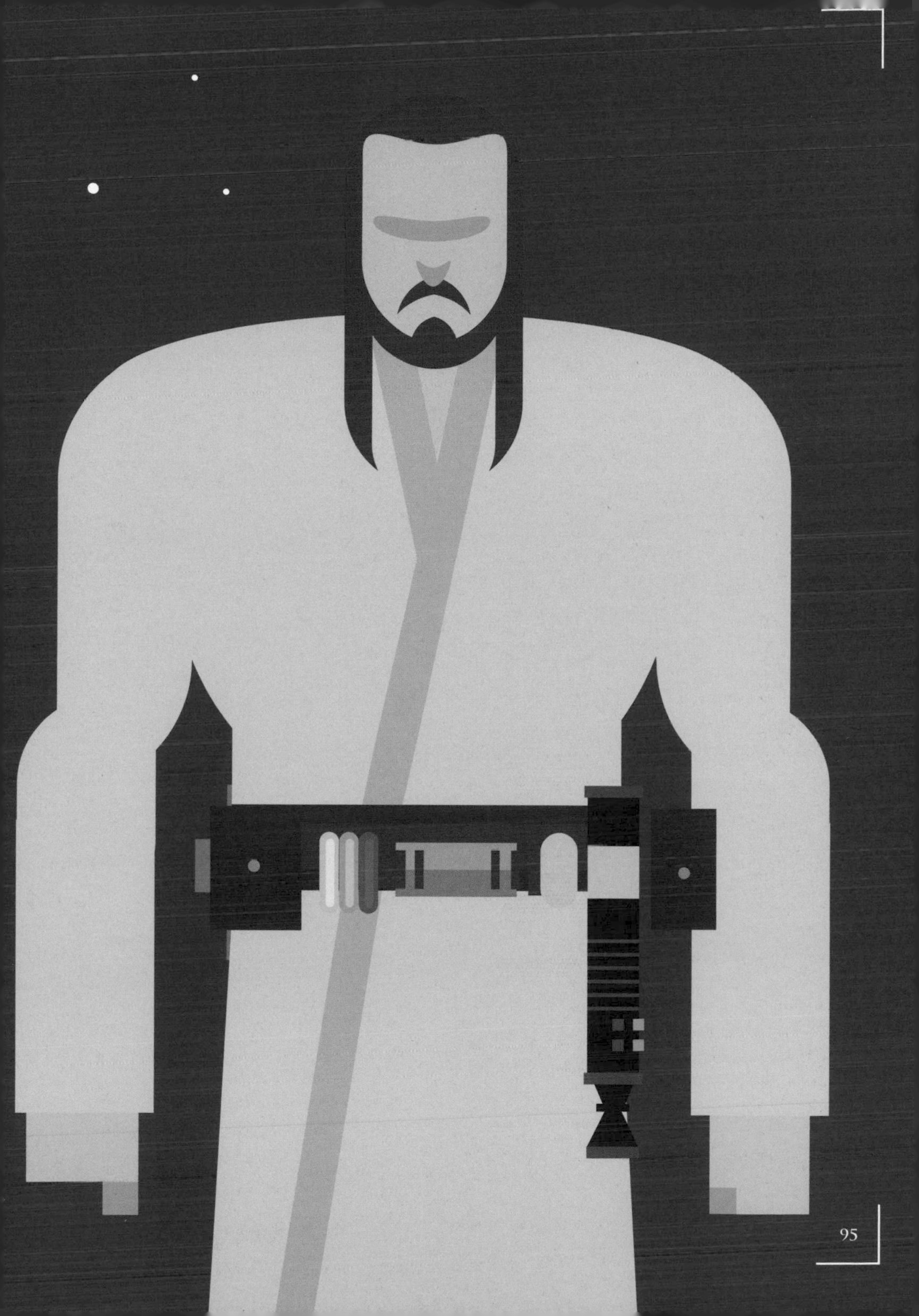

CHARA TER COSTUMES THROU H THE FILMS

DARTH VADER [total : 1]

Ep. IV : 1
Ep. V : 1
Ep. VI : 1

OBI-WAN KENOBI [total : 1]

Ep. IV : 1
Ep. V : 1

CHEWBACCA TOTAL [total : 1]

Ep. IV : 1
Ep. V : 1
Ep. VI : 1

LUKE SKYWALKER [total : 12]

Ep. IV : 4 (Tatooine, stormtrooper, pilot, ceremony)
Ep. V : 5 (Hoth, pilot, Dagobah, Bespin, sickbay)
Ep. VI : 3 (Jedi, pilot, Endor)

HAN SOLO [total : 10]

Ep. IV : 3 (classic, stormtrooper, ceremony)
Ep. V : 3 (Hoth, Bespin, carbonite)
Ep. VI : 4 (carbonite, Jabba, Endor, final)

LEIA [total : 11]

Ep. IV : 3 (classic, Yavin 4, ceremony)
Ep. V : 3 (Hoth, Bespin, sickbay)
Ep. VI : 5 (Boushh, slave, Endor, Ewok, final)

LANDO [total : 3]

Ep. V : 1 (Bespin)
Ep. VI : 2 (Jabba, classic)

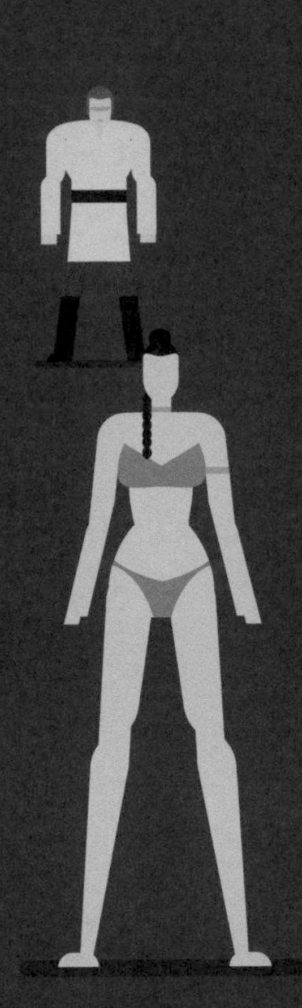

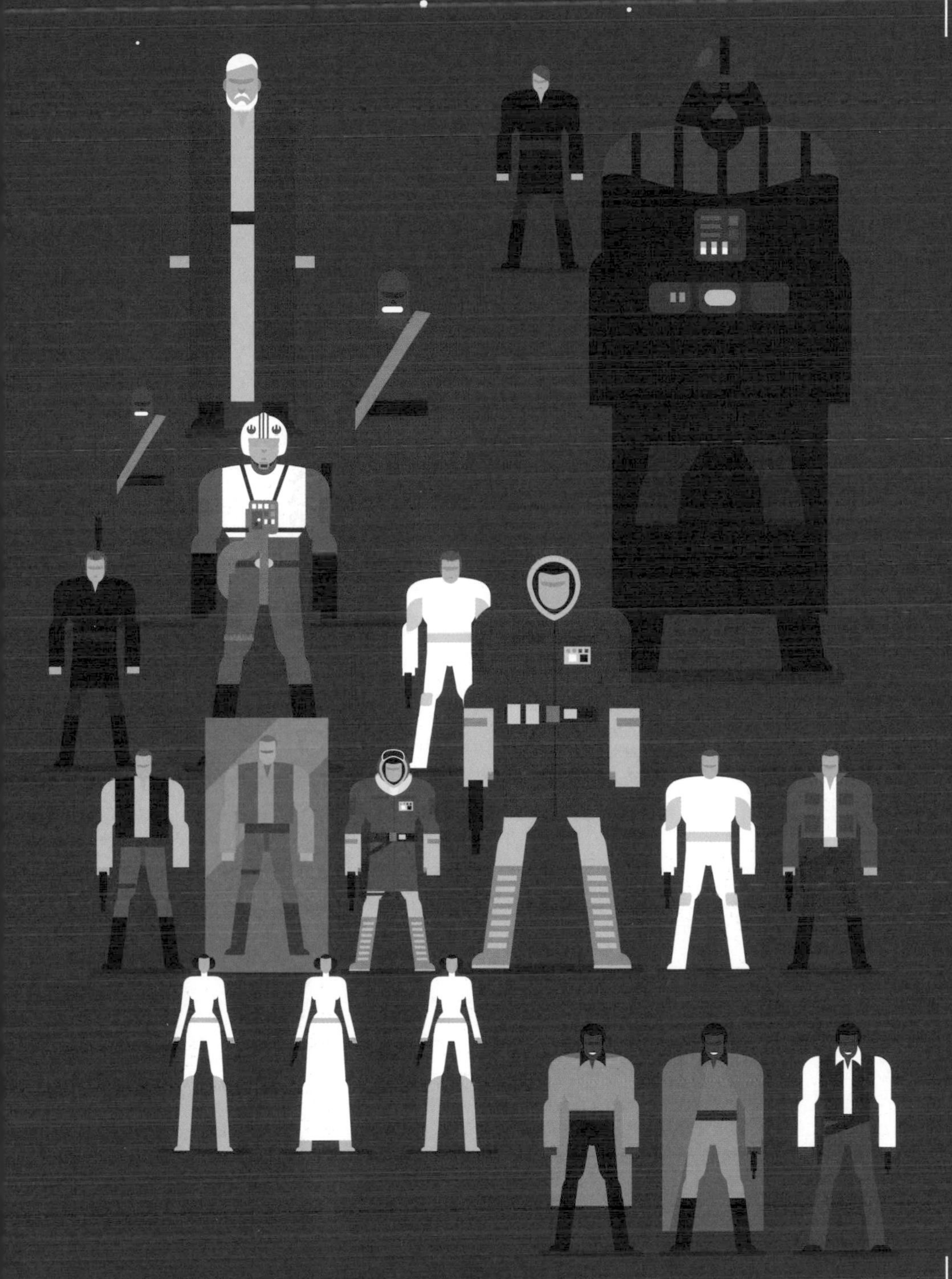

SECOND TRILOGY

[1999-2005]

CHARACTER HEIGHT

Padmé Amidala
1.65m

Darth Maul
1.75m

Obi-Wan Kenobi
1.79m

Anakin Skywalker
1.85m

Yoda
66cm

Mace Windu
1.88m

Qui-G
1.9

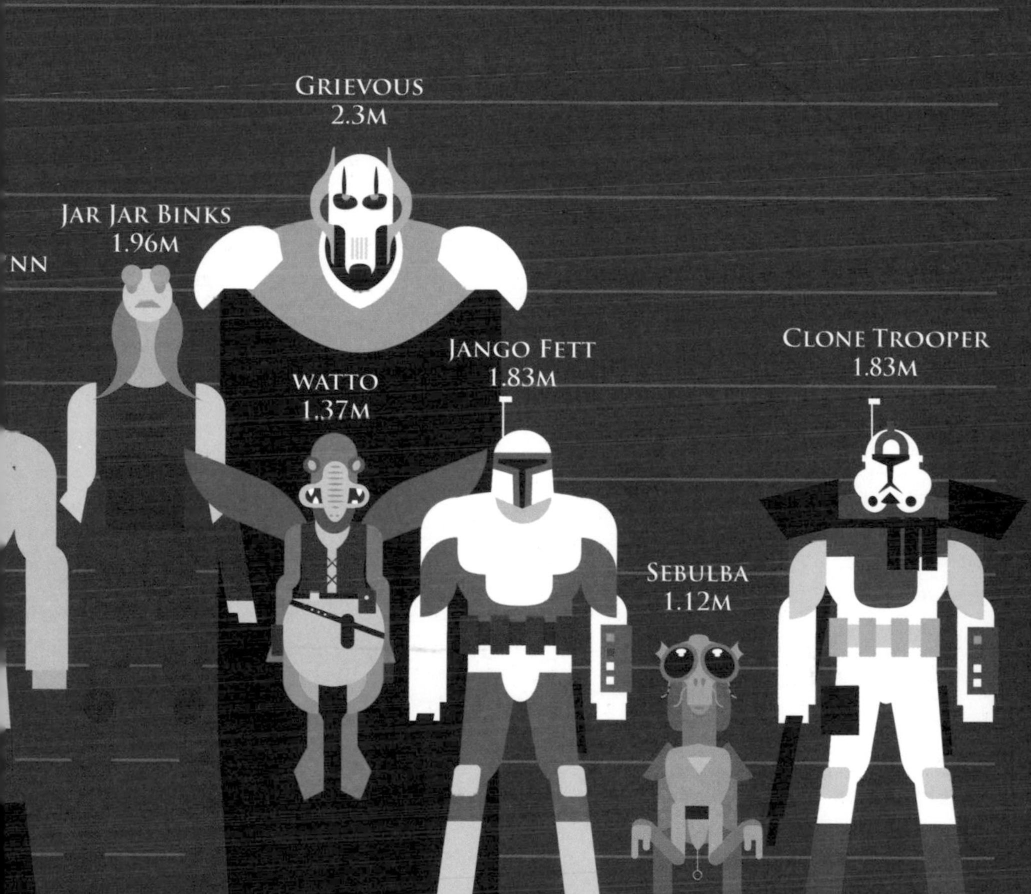

NN

JAR JAR BINKS
1.96M

GRIEVOUS
2.3M

WATTO
1.37M

JANGO FETT
1.83M

SEBULBA
1.12M

CLONE TROOPER
1.83M

CHARACTER JOURNEYS

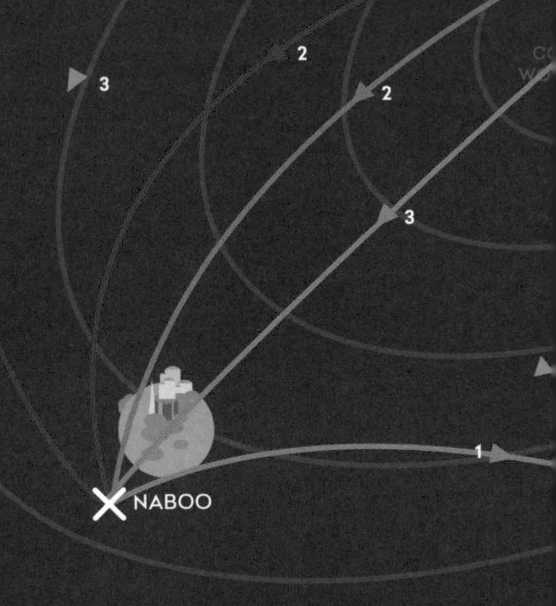

MID RIM

FELUCIA

EXPANSION REGION

INNER RIM

COLONIES

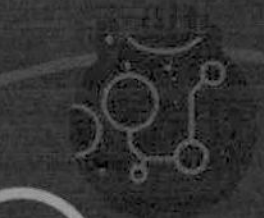

CORUSCANT

ALDERAAN

INNER CLUSTER

KASHYYYK

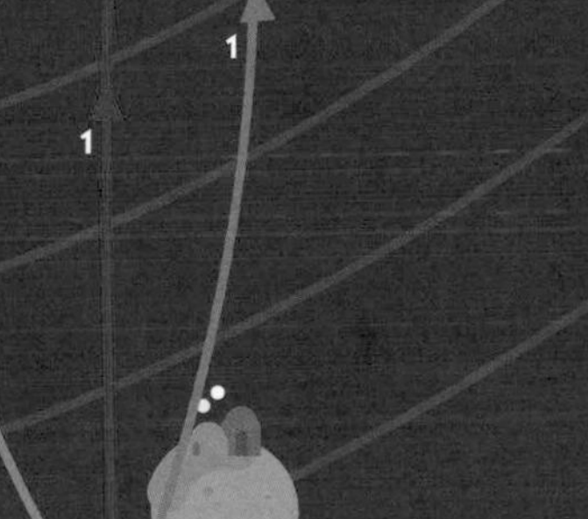

KAMINO

TATOOINE

1

GEONOSIS

ANAKIN SKYWALKER 

PADMÉ AMIDALA 

OBI-WAN KENOBI 

C-3PO 

R2-D2 

YODA 

PALPATINE 

BOONTA RACE IN 32 BBY RACE RESULTS

ANAKIN SKYWALKER

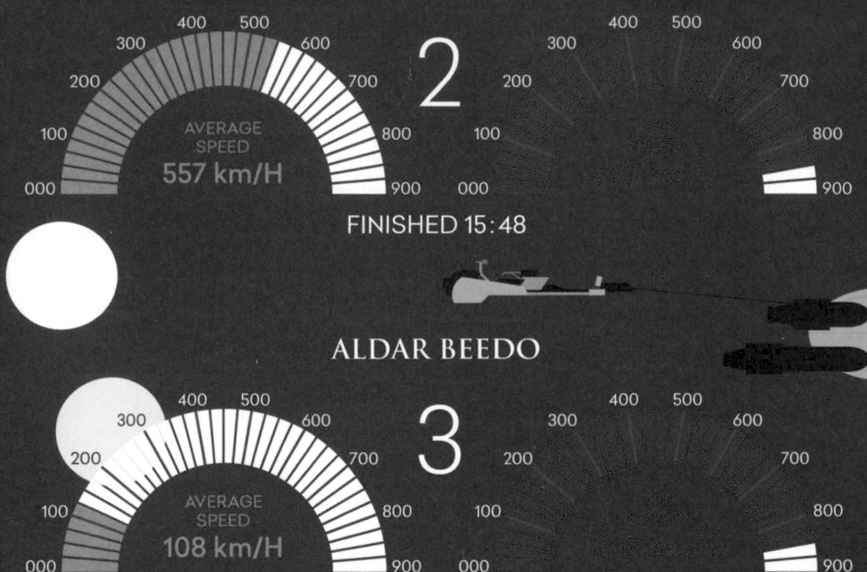

FINISHED 15:52

ACCIDENTS/ELIMINATION

NEVA KEE, RATTS TYERELL, SEBULBA, ARK ROOSE, WAN SANDAGE, MARS GUO, MAWHONIC, DUD BOLT, CLEGG HOLDFAST, ODY MANDRELL, TEEMTO PAGALIES, BEN QUADINAROS

EBE ENDOCOTT

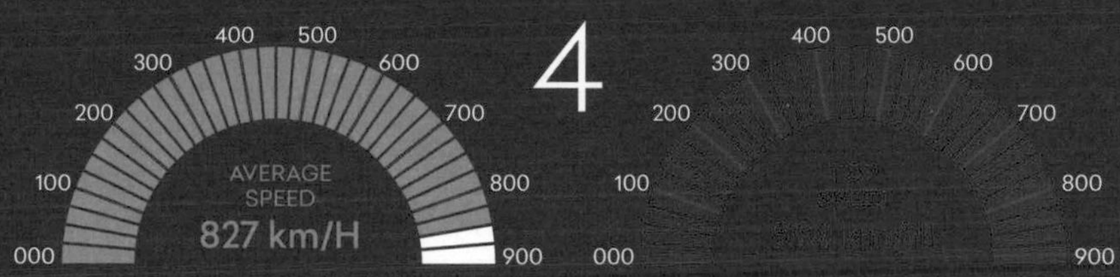

FINISHED 16:04

ELAN MAK

AVERAGE
SPEED
737 km/H

FINISHED 16:10

BOLES ROOR

FINISHED 16:42

PODRACERS

Mars Guo
Yellow, green, silver
7.24m/790 km/h
2 Plug-2 Behemoth

Aldar Beedo
Light blue, yellow
10.59m/823 km/h
2 turbo jets
Mark IV Flat-Twin

Dud Bolt
Metal, orange
7.92m/760 km/h
2 engines

Neva Kee
Sky blue, white
7.16m/785 km/h
2 engines

Gasgano
Yellow
6.71m/823 km/h
2 engines

RATTS TYERELL

SEBULBA
Orange
7.47m/829 km/h
2 Collor Pondrat
Plug-F Mammoth Split-X

MAWHONIC
Lemon yellow
3.81m/775 km/h
2 engines

WAN SANDAGE
Beige
5.03m/785 km/h

CLEGG HOLDFAST
Metal, red
10.36m/800 km/h
2 engines

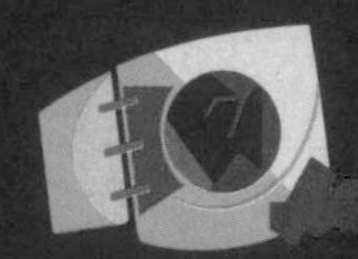

Teemto Pagalies
Metal, green, orange
10.67m/775 km/h
2 Long Tail IPG-X1131

Ark "Bumpy" Roose

Ody Mandrell
Metal, red
8.69m/790 km/h
2 XL 5115

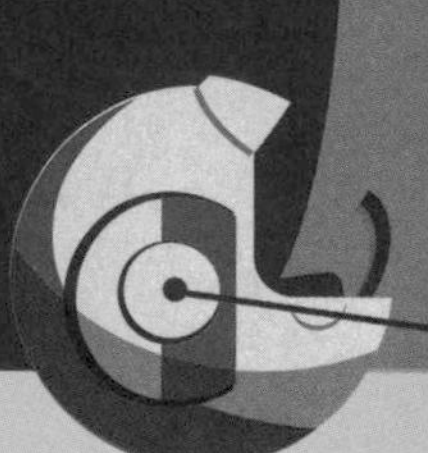

Elan Mak
Light gray,
orange, cream
3.81m/420 km/h
2 KRT 410C

Ben Quadrinos
Red, metal
4.5m/940 km/h
4 engines

Anakin Skywalker
Yellow
7m/947 km/h
2 Radon-Ulzer 620C engines

Boles Roor
Rust, light yellow
7.39m/790 km/h
2 904E 4-barrel Quadrijets

Ebe Endocott
Light turquoise, light orange
9.55m/785 km/h
2 J930 Dash-8

FINAL BATTLE

Locations: Plain on Naboo /Palace of Naboo /Theed generator /Space – Vuutun Palaa

Length/Beginning : 1.45.06 **End:** 2.04.18 = 19.12 minutes

What's at stake: stopping the Trade Federation's invasion of Naboo

Beginning: Federation fires on the Gungans at 1.46.12

Forces present: Gungans vs droid army /Amidala vs Federation /Jedi vs Sith /Naboo fleet vs Federation vessel

Key characters

Republic

Jar Jar Binks | Roos Tarpals | Padmé Amidala | Panaka

Jedi

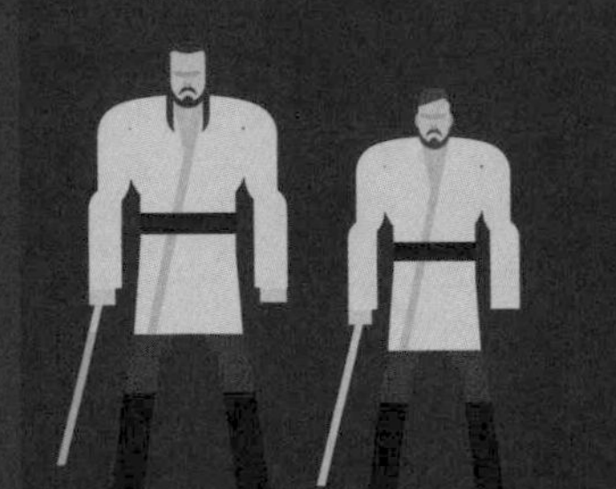

Qui-Gon Jinn | Obi-Wan Kenobi | Anakin Skywalker

Sith

Darth Maul

Federation

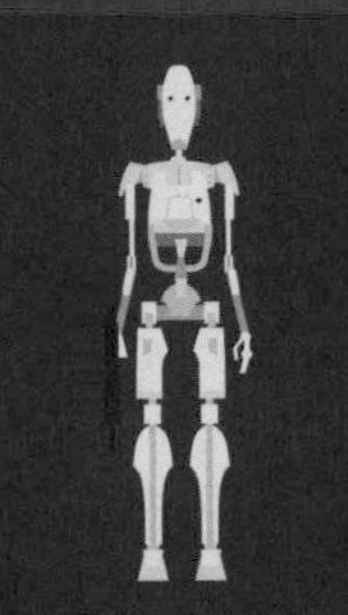

Droids

1) Chronology and Events:
Plain of Naboo

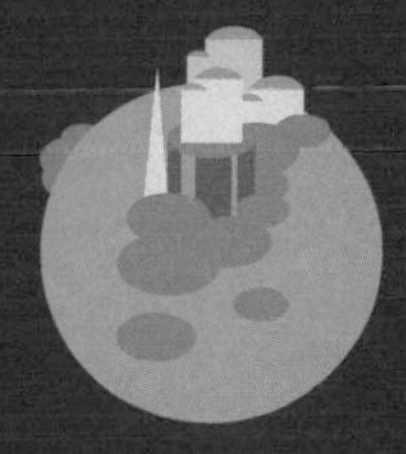

Federation's first shot at 1.46.12

Droids deployed at 1.49.16

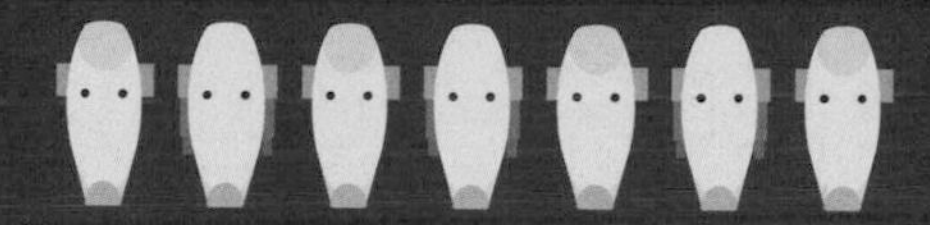

Droids cross the Gungan shield at 1.49.41

Destruction of the Gungan shield at 1.56.48

Jar Jar and Roos Tarpals are surrounded at 2.00.23

Droids annihilated at 2.03.36

In Brief

NUMBER OF DROIDS ON THE GROUND :
10 MTT =
1000+ droids (one MTT = 112 droids or 20 droidekas)

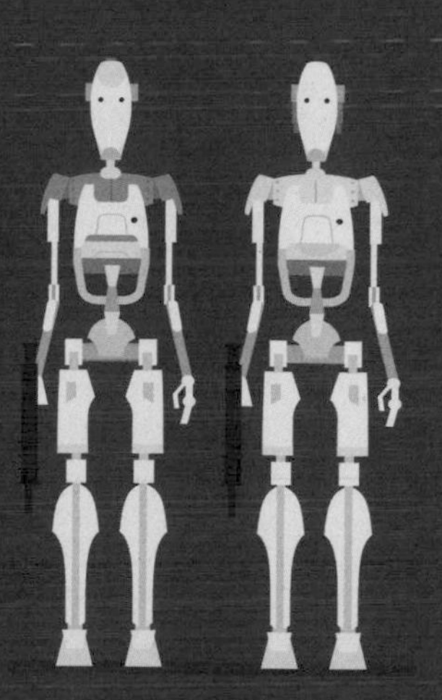

JAR JAR'S GAFFES

- falls off mount at 1.49.51
- taken out by his own cannonball at 1.50.04
- panic attack at 1.53.26
- gets his foot stuck in a wire at 1.53.33
- picks off 3 droids by accident at 1.53.37
- hides under a vehicle which starts to move at 1.57.03
- accidentally releases explosive cannonballs at 1.57.17
- tries to outrun explosive cannonballs at 1.57.28
- lands on the barrel of an AAT at 1.57.45
- fails to catch a grenade which destroys a droid at 1.57.56
- surrenders like a coward at 2.00.28

2) CHRONOLOGY AND EVENTS:
PALACE OF NABOO – THEED HANGAR

Arrival of Amidala and the Jedi at the Palace of Naboo (in Federation hands) at 1.46.19

Arrival at the Theed Hangar at 1.47.05

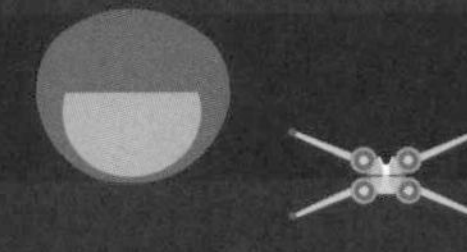

Anakin boards a fighter at 1.47.45

Darth Maul appears at 1.50.26

Droidekas arrive at 1.50.48

Anakin wipes out the droidekas at 1.51.38

Amidala and Panaka go out the window at 1.55.05

Queen's decoy appears at 2.00.48
TURNING POINT

First shot against a Federation AAT at 1.46.38

Naboo fighters lift at 1.47.32

First loss for Naboo: a fighter at 1.47.58

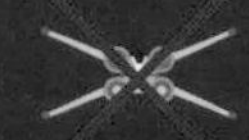

Amidala's troops split off at 1.50.44

Anakin powers up his fighter at 1.51.25

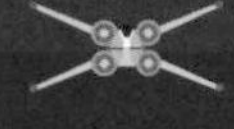

Anakin lifts at 1.51.56

Amidala and Panaka arrested at 1.58.26

Amidala retakes control of the palace at 2.01.14

3) CHRONOLOGY AND EVENTS:
THEED HANGAR – THEED GENERATOR

Darth Maul ignites his lightsaber at 1.51.02

Obi-Wan and Qui-Go ignite theirs at 1.51.

Interruption of combat at 1.56.21

Obi-Wan resumes the fight at 2.01.30

Obi-Wan falls into the pit and loses his lightsaber at 02.02.10

Cuts Darth Maul in two at 2.04.18

Qui-Gon is run through at 1.59.55
TURNING POINT

Obi-Wan breaks Darth Maul's lightsaber at 2.01.45

Obi-Wan recovers Qui-Gon's lightsaber at 2.04.17

In Brief

Number of lightsaber clashes: 115

4) Chronology and Events:
Space – Droid Control Centre

Fighter fleet arrives within range of the Vuutun Palaa: 1.48.07

First shots exchanged at 1.48.20 (Naboo green, Federation red)

Anakin closes on the Vuutun Palaa at 1.53.10

Anakin lands in the Vuutun Palaa at 1.59.00

Anakin restarts his fighter at 2.02.25
TURNING POINT

Destruction of a core on Vuutun Palaa at 2.02.40

Anakin escapes from the Vuutun Palaa at 2.03.20

Vuutun Palaa explodes at 2.03.20

CHARACTER JOURNEYS

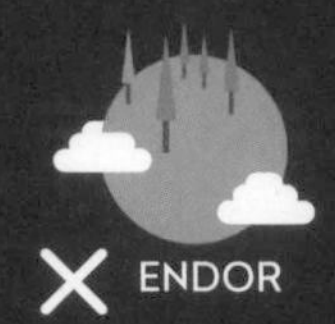

OUTER RIM

1

1

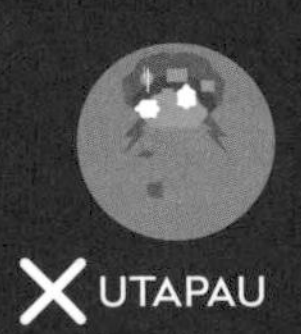

2

2

YAVIN 4

MID RIM

EXPANSION REGION

FELUCIA

INNER RIM

COLONIES

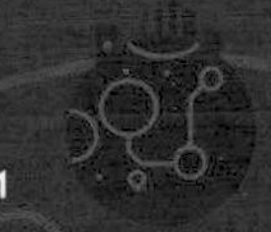

CORUSCANT

ALDERAAN

INNER CLUSTER

KASHYYYK

KAMINO

TATOOINE

GEONOSIS

ANAKIN SKYWALKER 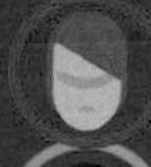

PADMÉ AMIDALA 

OBI-WAN KENOBI 

C-3PO 

R2-D2 

YODA 

PALPATINE 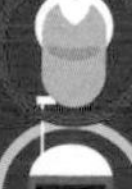

JANGO FETT 

Final Battle

Locations: Geonosis : Petranaki arena /air and land /Dooku's hangar

Length/Beginning : 1.50.03 **End :** 2.10.51 = 20.48 minutes

What's at stake: destruction of a droid foundry and arrest of Count Dooku

Beginning: Windu ignites his lightsaber — **End:** Dooku escapes

Forces present: Clone army commanded by Yoda and Jedi council commanded by Windu vs Separatists commanded by Dooku

Key characters

Republic

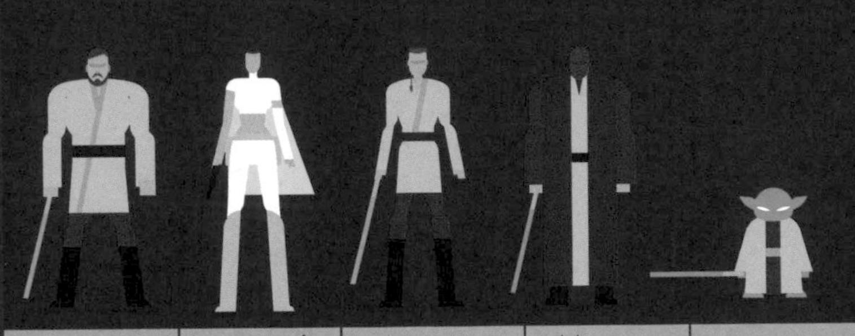

Obi-Wan Kenobi	Padmé Amidala	Anakin Skywalker	Mace Windu	Yoda

Separatists

Jango Fett	Count Dooku

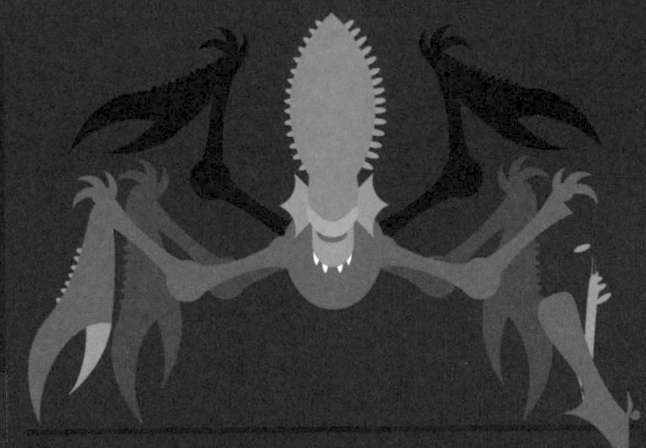

1) Chronology and Events:
Geonosis: Petranaki arena

Mace Windu ignites his lightsaber at 1.50.03

Jedi Council joins the battle at 1.50.14

Separatists open fire at 1.50.42

Jango Fett attacks with a flamethrower at 1.50.45

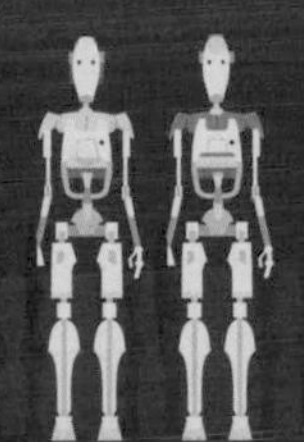

Droid army appears at 1.50.52

Anakin and Obi-Wan recover their lightsabers at 1.51.06

Jango Fett kills a Jedi (Coleman Trebor) at 1.52.28

Mace Windu beheads Jango Fett at 1.53.19

Combat interrupted at 1.55.33

Yoda and the clone army join the battle at 1.56.27
TURNING POINT

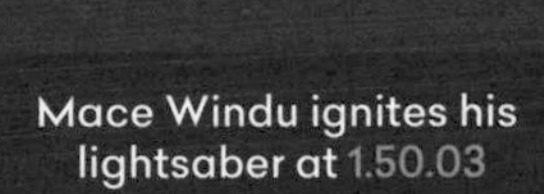

In brief

JEDI IN THE ARENA: 20
7 fallen in combat

Number of shots fired by C-3PO: 15

Jango Fett — Reek

Reek gores Jango at 1.52.54
Reek tramples Jango at 1.52.58
Jango kills reek at 1.53.08

Obi-Wan Kenobi — Acklay

Obi-Wan kills acklay at 1.54.39
Boba Fett recovers Jango Fett's helmet at 1.57.45

2) Chronology and events:
Petranaki arena: air/ground

Destruction of a Geonosis reservoir at 1.58.13

Destruction of a LAAT/i at 1.58.54

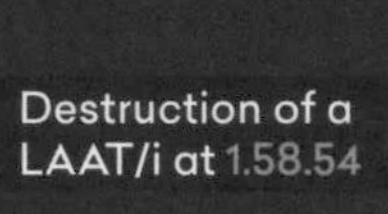

Mace Windu takes command on the ground at 1.59.08

Yoda takes command in the air at 1.59.17

Dooku escapes with the plans to the Death Star at 2.01.53

Destruction of a Federation vessel at 2.02.38

Anakin and Obi-Wan pursue Dooku at 2.03.16

Amidala falls from the LAAT/i at 2.03.35

Dooku arrives at his hangar at 2.04.36

Anakin and Obi-Wan reach the hangar at 2.04.45

Amidala regains consciousness at 2.06.02

In Brief

First appearance of the Death Star at 1.58.28 in Dooku's command center

3) Chronology and Events:
Dooku's hangar

Dooku knocks Anakin down with Force lightning at 2.05.06

Obi-Wan blocks lightning with his lightsaber at 2.05.20

Dooku ignites his lightsaber at 2.05.30

Anakin regains consciousness at 2.05.55

Dooku wounds Obi-Wan at 2.06.29

Anakin saves Obi-Wan at 2.06.39

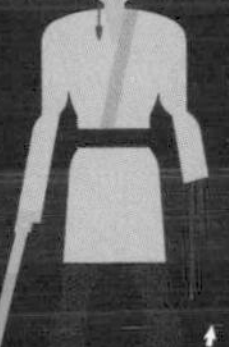

Anakin has two lightsabers at 2.06.50

Dooku disarms the green lightsaber at 2.06.57

Dooku cuts off Anakin's arm at 2.07.30

Yoda appears at 2.07.46
TURNING POINT

Yoda reflects Dooku's Force lightning at 2.08.46

Dooku ignites his lightsaber at 2.09.07

Yoda ignites his at 2.09.18

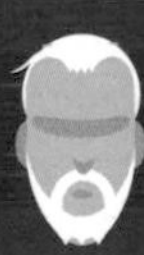

Dooku topples a tank at 2.10.00

Yoda saves Obi-Wan and Anakin at 2.10.15

Amidala reaches the hangar at 2.10.40

Dooku escapes at 2.10.41

In brief

NUMBER OF CLASHES: 42 (Obi-Wan/Anakin/Dooku) – 28 (Yoda/Dooku)
PROJECTILES DEFLECTED BY YODA: 5
LEAPS PERFORMED BY YODA: 18 in 42 seconds = a leap every 2.33 seconds

CHARACTER JOURNEYS

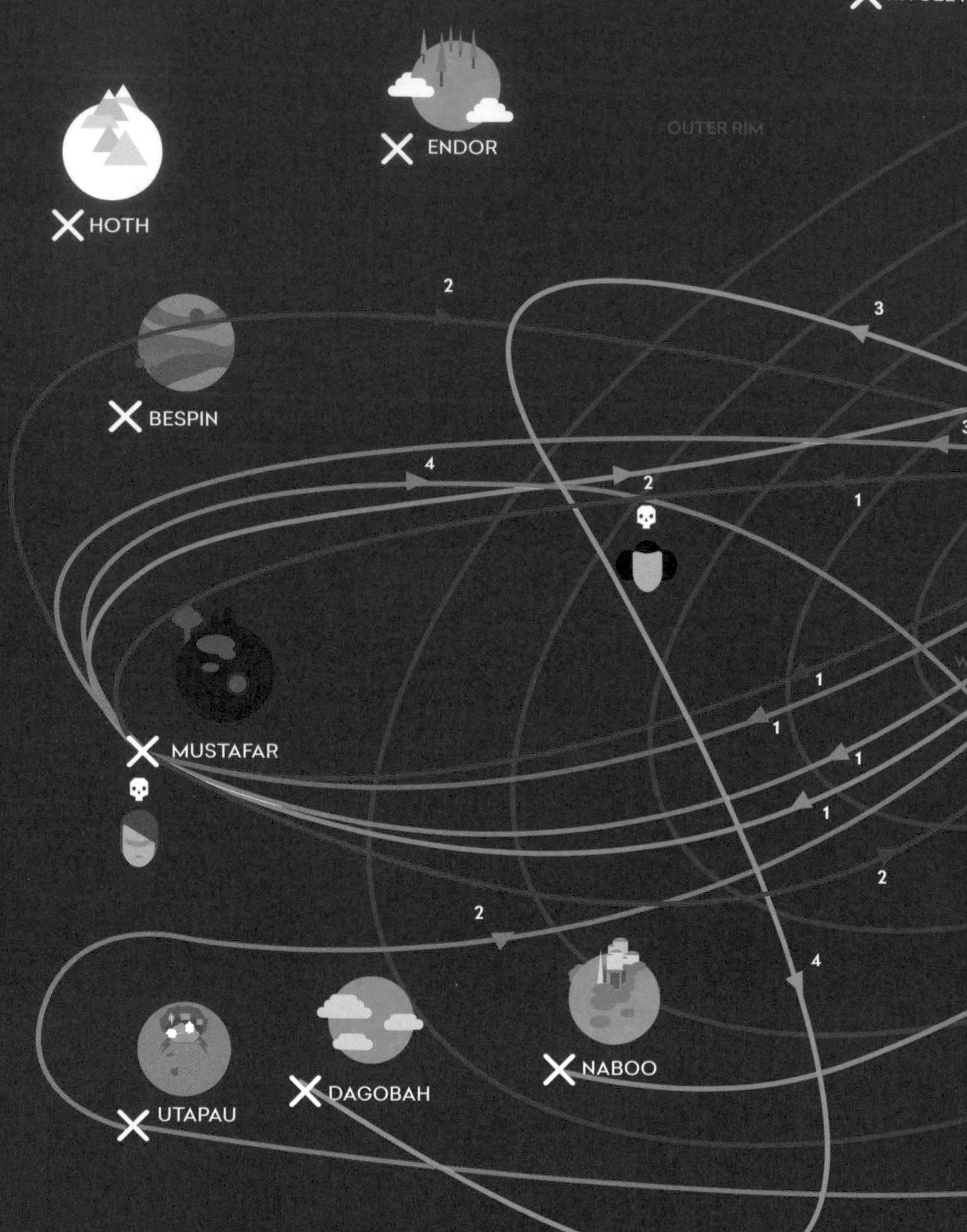

MID RIM

EXPANSION REGION

FELUCIA

INNER RIM

COLONIES

CORUSCANT

ALDERAAN

2

1

1

KASHYYYK

1

5

KAMINO

3

TATOOINE

GEONOSIS

Anakin Skywalker

Padmé Amidala

Obi-Wan Kenobi

C-3PO

R2-D2

Yoda

Leia

Palpatine

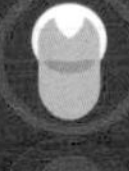

Luke Skywalker

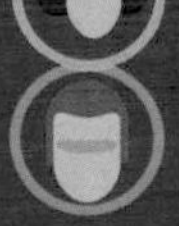

Chewbacca

FINAL BATTLE

LOCATION : Mustafar / Coruscant

LENGTH/BEGINNING: 1.46.04 END: 1.59.37 = 13.33 minutes

BEGINNING: appearance of Obi-Wan

END: Anakin's legs cut off/Yoda falls

FORCES PRESENT: Jedi VS Sith

KEY CHARACTERS

REPUBLIC

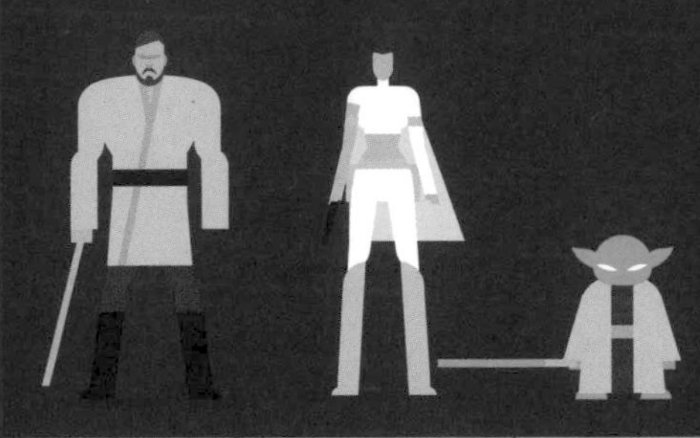

OBI-WAN KENOBI | PADMÉ AMIDALA | YODA

SITH

DARTH SIDIOUS

IN TRANSITION

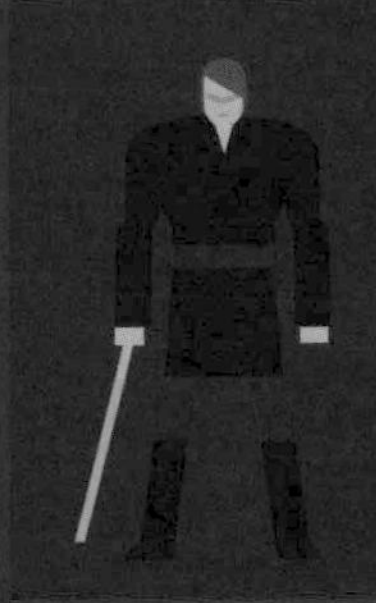

ANAKIN SKYWALKER

1) CHRONOLOGY AND EVENTS: MUSTAFAR

Obi-Wan appears at 1.46.04

Anakin Force-chokes Amidala at 1.46.17

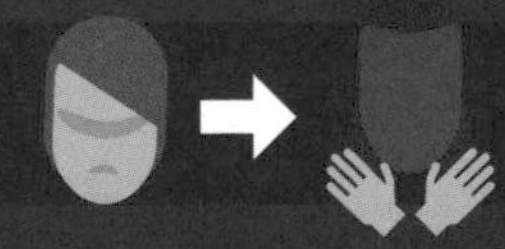

Anakin drops his cloak at 1.46.46

Obi-Wan drops his cloak at 1.46.51

Obi-Wan ignites first at 1.47.53

Anakin ignites at 1.47.54

First clash at 1.47.56

they go indoors

Anakin strangles Obi-Wan at 1.50.57

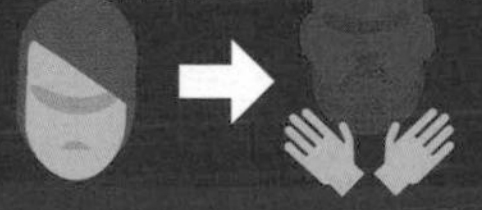

Force vs Force at 1.52.04

Steam pipes at 1.52.18

outdoors

Obi-Wan lands on the river of lava at 1.57.37

Anakin lands on the river of lava at 1.57.55

Obi-Wan leaps from his platform, returns to solid ground and gains the upper hand at 1.59.16
TURNING POINT

Anakin leaps off his platform at 1.59.35

Obi-Wan cuts off Anakin's arm and legs at 1.59.37

In brief

LIGHTSABER CLASHES:
168

KICKS:
7

2) Chronology and Events:
Under the Senate/In the Senate

Yoda arrives in front of Sidious by knocking down two Imperial guards at 1.48.18

Sidious strikes Yoda down with Force lightning at 1.48.52

Mas Amedda leaves the scene at 1.49.32

Yoda opens an eye at 1.49.45

Yoda strikes down Sidious at 1.50.02

Yoda ignites his lightsaber at 1.50.24

Sidious ignites at 1.50.31

Sidious and Yoda move into the Senate at 1.51.30

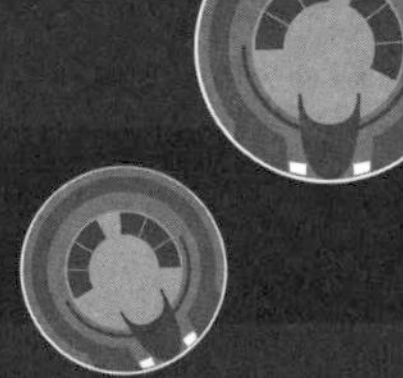

Sidious bombards Yoda with Senate seats at 1.52.44

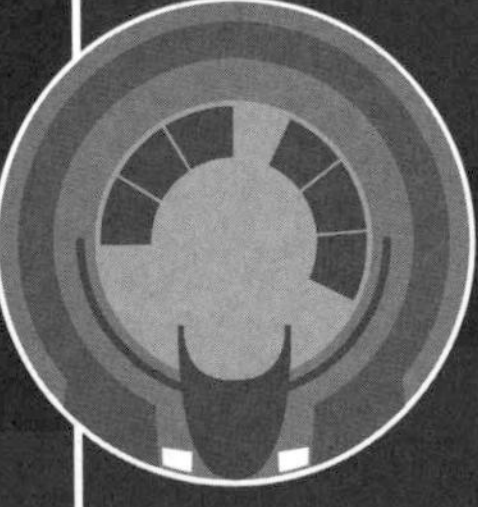

Yoda extinguishes his lightsaber at 1.53.08

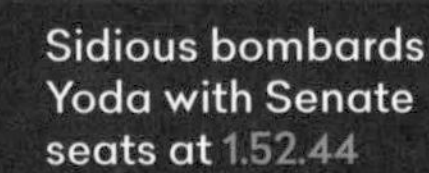

Yoda reignites his lightsaber at 1.53.31

Sidious disarms Yoda with Force lightning at 1.53.36
TURNING POINT

BOOM!

Lightning duel at 1.53.36

Force explosion at 1.53.52

BOOM!

BOOM!

Yoda falls at 1.54.05

IN BRIEF

LIGHTSABER CLASHES : 40

DARTH SIDIOUS

LEAPS PERFORMED : 2

YODA

LEAPS PERFORMED : 24
PROJECTILES AVOIDED: 6
PROJECTILE RETURNED: 1

CHARACTER COSTUMES THROUGH THE FILMS

Obi-Wan Kenobi [total : 1]

Ep. I : 1
Ep. II : 1
Ep. III : 1

Qui-Gon Jinn [total : 1]

Ep. I : 1

Anakin Skywalker [total : 6]

Ep. I : 3
Ep. II : 2
Ep. III : 1

Padmé Amidala [total : 36]

Ep.I : 10
Ep. II : 15
Ep. III : 11

Jar-Jar Binks [total : 3]

Ep. I : 1
Ep. II : 1
Ep. III : 1

Palpatine [total : 12]

Ep. I : 2
Ep. II : 3
Ep. III : 7

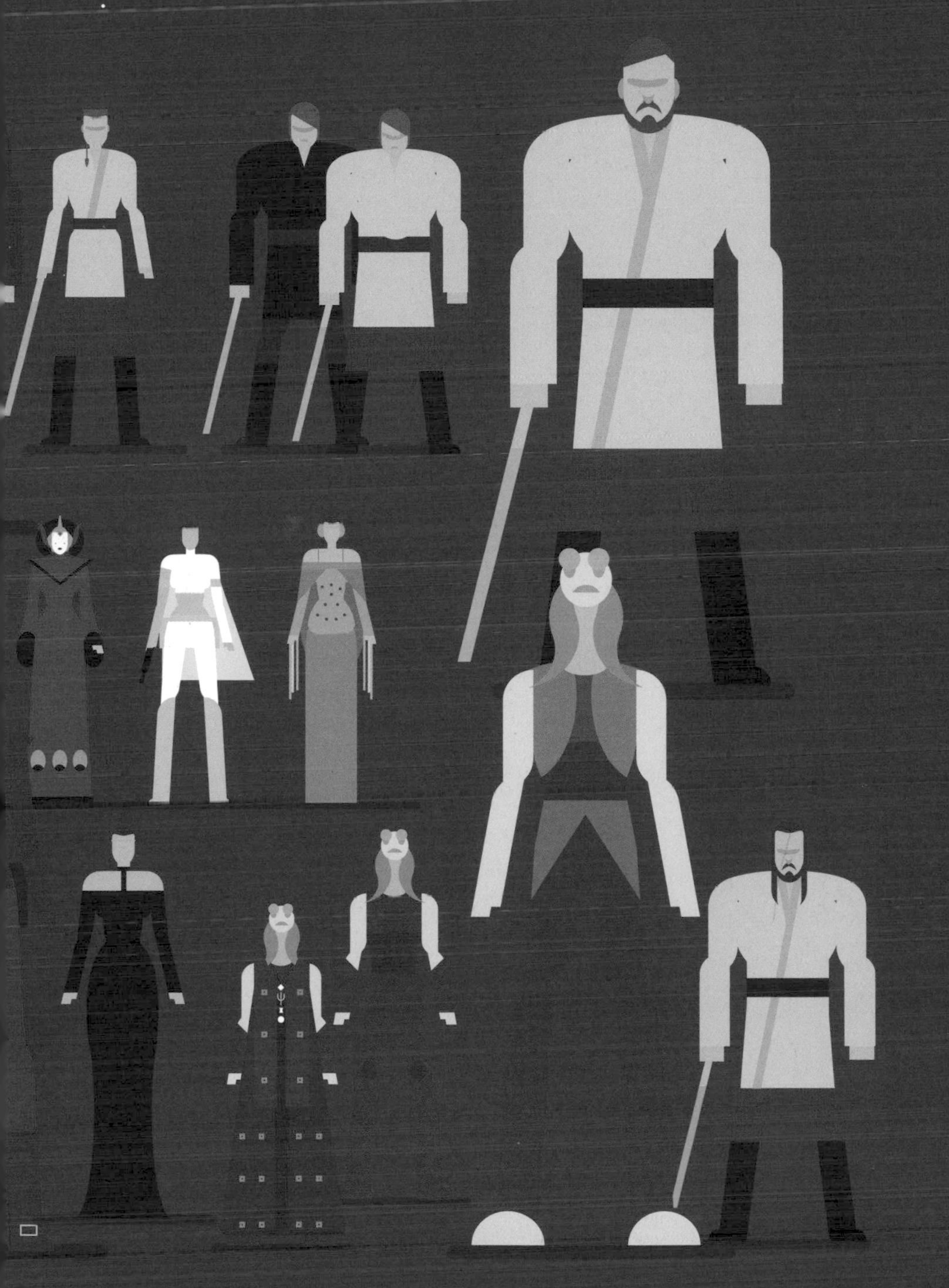